MENDING FATE

THE SCOTTISH BILLIONAIRE BOOK 3

M. S. PARKER

BELMONTE PUBLISHING, LLC

THE SCOTTISH BILLIONAIRE READING ORDER

Thank you for reading *Mending Fate*, the final book in my series, *The Scottish Billionaire*. I highly recommend reading the books in this order:

Prequel – The Scottish Billionaire

1. Off Limits

2. Breaking Rules

3. Mending Fate

ONE
ALEC

When I'd woken this morning, I'd felt like everything had changed. Some of it made me uneasy, but in other ways, it was as if a weight had been lifted.

I had told Evanne last night about my dyslexia and explained that the mistakes on her homework had been my fault. It seemed that Lumen had been right when she said that a good portion of the reason Evanne had been upset had been because she hadn't understood what happened. Telling my daughter the truth hadn't made me any less in her eyes. In fact, she'd hugged me and told me that she loved me.

I had spent my entire life focused on making money to improve the lives of those I loved. When Evanne was born, she had simply shifted my focus to her being the most important person in my world. Now, I saw that I could have so much more. Not only a relationship with my daughter but also one with a woman I could see myself with for a long time to come.

Perhaps forever.

The fact that I could even think *forever* just proved how much I had changed over the last couple months.

Forever could wait, however. Right now, I needed to pick up Evanne from school. I smiled at the thought of *mo chride*, with her long dark brown curls and blue eyes.

"Mr. McCrae." My assistant, Tuesday, appeared in my doorway. "You asked me to remind you about leaving a few minutes early so you wouldn't get caught in traffic again."

"Aye, thank you." I closed my desk drawer.

"You're a good father, you know." She smiled warmly before heading back to her desk.

I really hoped she was right because I intended to see a lawyer tomorrow regarding a new custody agreement. After I talked to Evanne last night, I'd sat down with Keli and explained that our short experiment hadn't worked. She and I would never be the family she wanted us to be.

At least she'd taken it better than I thought she would. No tears or yelling. Just a simple, "If you're sure that's how you feel," before she'd headed to the guest room she'd been using. I supposed she'd be more upset once it sank in that it wasn't a family, in general, I was rejecting. It was just a family with her.

I'd wait to tell her that I'd invited Lumen to move in with me until after I'd gotten all the legal custody issues out of the way. No need to rock that particular boat.

First, I intended to speak to Evanne about how things would be now that her mom was back in Seattle. That was a conversation best had over pizza. We'd stop for her favorite on our way home. I took a moment in the school parking lot to place my order.

Once that was done, I went inside with a handful of other parents and staff who were here for their children or their charges. Judging by some of the looks I received, questions were still circulating about what had happened to Vice Principal Cornelius Harvey during the meeting two weeks ago, and my name was linked to the incident.

Then again, it might have been something more than that. Who knew how much anyone here knew about Lumen and me seeing each other...or about the way we'd first met.

I frowned as I remembered one of the things Lumen said last night during our argument. Principal McKenna and the vice principal knew that Lumen had once worked at a massage parlor. Granted, she'd shown them that she had put Real Life Bodywork on her resumé, and then she'd explained that it was a legitimate business, but that didn't mean someone hadn't spread all sorts of rumors.

Someone. There was only one person who would do something like that...Cornelius Harvey, the school's vice principal.

The man was a first-rate bastard.

I pushed thoughts of him out of my head and smiled as I reached Lumen's classroom. The chaos of kids swept past me, and I scanned them for Evanne. She was tall for her age, which should have made her easy to see, but she wasn't with them. That didn't surprise me, though. Evanne liked her teacher as much as she did her classmates.

Speaking of Evanne's teacher...

My eyes met Lumen's, and her entire face lit up. I went a few steps into the classroom, and that was when her expression shifted to one of puzzlement.

Dammit, Keli.

"I came to pick up Evanne, but based on your face, I'm going to guess that Keli already did and neglected to tell me."

I blew out a long, frustrated breath. Somehow, I didn't think this was a mere slip on Keli's part. More likely, she hadn't been as accepting as I'd thought, and she was trying to make my life miserable now that she knew she wouldn't be the part of it she wanted to be.

The concern on Lumen's face deepened. "Alec, what are you talking about? No one picked Evanne up. She didn't come to school today."

I frowned. "What are you saying, lass?"

Lumen came over to me, lowering her voice so that the few remaining students around us couldn't hear what she had to say. "Keli called the office and said that Evanne wouldn't be in today. I assumed she was sick."

"I had an early meeting, so I asked Keli to bring Evanne this morning. She didn't say anything about Evanne being sick." The sinking feeling in my stomach told me that this was worse than her simply not telling me that Evanne had taken ill. Something was wrong.

My phone buzzed just as Lumen's phone rang, and we both reached for them, hoping that at least one of them would have answers for us.

"Brie? What's wrong?"

That didn't sound like anything that had to do with Evanne, but the text on my phone certainly did.

I'm assuming by now you know that Evanne isn't at school. I refuse to lose my daughter just because you found someone different you want to fuck. When you come back to your senses, we can discuss things again.

"Fuck, Keli. What did you do?" I muttered as I hit the option to call her back.

It went straight to voicemail.

No surprise there.

"Keli, what the hell do you think you're doing? If you want to talk things out, then we do that, but this is not the way. Call me, and we'll meet."

I hung up just as Lumen turned toward me, her face pale. "Soleil's missing."

Something in her voice told me I should know who Soleil was, but I had more important things on my mind. "I think Keli took Evanne somewhere."

Lumen appeared equally distracted. "Brie can't find Soleil anywhere. She didn't go to school today, and no one knows where she is."

"What are you talking about?" I barely stopped myself from yelling at her.

"Soleil's the foster girl I've been spending time with." Lumen blinked, her hand coming up to cover her forehead. "Sorry. It's just that she's been going through a lot lately, and Brie's worried."

"What?" Had Lumen gone daft? My child was missing, and she didn't care? "Keli *took my daughter.*"

Lumen frowned. "Evanne's with her mom, so she's okay, right? I mean, Keli's not dangerous or anything."

I scowled. "That's not the point. Evanne is supposed to be here and then home. With me."

"Look, I don't have the time to do this," Lumen said, her tone dismissive. "I have to go find Soleil."

"I don't care about some runaway!" I snapped, vaguely aware that people were looking at us. "We have to find Evanne!"

The look of shock on Lumen's face should have given me pause, but it didn't. She was worried about some girl she barely knew when Keli could have taken Evanne anywhere. How could she not see what was more important?

"Soleil could be in real danger." Lumen's voice was soft, but the look she gave me was piercing. "At least Evanne is safe with Keli. I'm not saying you shouldn't look for Evanne, but *I* have to find Soleil."

What was she saying?

"I dinnae care about some random girl. I care about my daughter, and I canna understand why you're all worked up over this near-stranger." I shoved my phone back in my pocket. "Finding Evanne is the only thing important to me."

A thousand emotions passed over Lumen's face, and I couldn't read a single one of them.

"You want to know why I care?" Her azure eyes

glinted with something fierce and foreign. "I care because Soleil doesn't have a family to make her their top priority, and I know what that feels like." She turned and grabbed her bag off the desk. "Not all of us have families, Alec."

And then she was gone.

TWO

LUMEN

I hated leaving like that, but I'd meant what I said. Soleil didn't have anyone else to make her the priority. Me not going with Alec didn't mean I wasn't worried about Evanne or that I didn't feel sick over how upset Alec was. I wanted him to find her. It was just that we both knew Keli wouldn't hurt their child, and there were so many people who could – and would – hurt Soleil.

Last week, Soleil had gotten caught stealing a pregnancy test, and she'd had security call me. After I'd picked her up, and she told me what she'd taken, I'd bought a test for her myself and waited while she took it. Fortunately, it had been negative. Right then, I'd made a promise to myself to find out who'd she'd been sleeping with, but I hadn't been able to get it out of her yet.

What if the guy was, as I'd feared, an adult? Could

he have convinced her to run away with him? I knew all too well how many kids in the foster system were trafficked that way. Some adult convinces a kid that they're loved, and that kid will do anything the adult wants.

Most of the time, that leads to the adult not only abusing the kid themselves but loaning the kid out to friends. From there, kids end up working the streets, being sold to other predators, forced into making pornography, and the majority never make it out alive.

My stomach churned, bile rising in my throat. I swallowed hard but didn't slow down. I needed to get to the bus stop before the bus left, or I'd have to wait twenty minutes until the next one came by. I'd given Soleil my address, so stopping by the apartment first made sense. During the ride, I'd make a list of places to check, places that most foster kids knew about, even if they'd never go there.

I'd been fortunate enough to make it through the system without being abused, and I'd never run away, but I wasn't naïve. I'd listened to other kids, remembered things they'd said.

I knew some places where desperate kids would go, places that even caseworkers and foster parents wouldn't know to look. I didn't even want to think about her being in any of those places, and I clung to the hope that when I arrived home, she'd be waiting for me.

But I knew I had to be realistic, which was why, even as I hoped, I made a mental list of the places I'd go and of how I'd get there. Having to rely on public transportation meant I needed to figure out the best ways to get different places based on how much I needed to walk and where the bus stops were.

Not for the first time, I wished I had a car. It would have made things much easier.

I was up on my feet the moment the bus rolled to a stop, slipping past the other passengers and hurrying down the stairs. I grimaced as a gust of wind blew cold rain into my face, but I didn't let it slow me down. My pace made my shoes pinch my toes, but that didn't slow me either. I needed to get home.

Soleil wasn't in the lobby when I arrived, and she wasn't in the hallway either. The moment I realized she wasn't sitting outside my apartment, the hope I'd allowed myself to feel died. I didn't bother trying to convince myself that Mai could have let Soleil inside.

Besides the fact that I knew Mai was at work and that she would have texted me the moment the girl showed up asking for me, I simply didn't have the energy to hope again, just to have it dashed in seconds. Roller-coaster emotions were a bitch.

When I opened the door, I was glad I'd made that decision because the apartment was dark and empty. I flipped on the light and kicked off my shoes, dropping my bags on the closest table. I stripped out of my dress clothes as I went and tossed them toward my laundry hamper when I entered my room. I grabbed a pair of jeans and a sweatshirt from my dresser, quickly dressing and putting together what I'd need.

Despite my desire to get going as quickly as possible, I knew I had to be smart about this. Whether Soleil had left under her own power or not, I needed to be prepared to deal with some unsavory people in unsavory places. That meant I needed money and protection.

I didn't have much of the first, but I gathered what I had. As for the latter, Mai and Hob had bought me a taser for Christmas the previous year. For legal reasons, I couldn't carry it to and from school, so I'd invested in pepper spray for my commute. Both were going with me.

Maybe I was overthinking this entire situation. I supposed it was possible that I could get a call any minute saying Soleil had shown up back at the home, or I'd find her simply walking around. I might never need any of the things I was putting into my bag, but if I did end up in a situation where any of them were necessary, I'd be glad to have them.

A couple bottles of water and some protein bars finished things off. I jotted a note to Mai, telling her what had happened, and that I didn't know when I'd be home, and then I started toward the door before stopping and turning back. I added a postscript in the hopes that she wouldn't completely freak out at the thought of me wandering around Seattle by myself at night.

P.S. DON'T FREAK OUT! I know what I'm doing.

Yeah, that should do it.

I slipped on my tennis shoes and headed back out into the shitty October weather. This was *not* going to be a fun way to spend the rest of my day.

At least if I was focused on trying to find Soleil, I wasn't thinking about how badly Alec's words had hurt me. He hadn't verbally attacked me, exactly. He'd been upset and worried about Evanne, so his reactions had been understandable, but that hadn't made the content any less painful.

He'd dismissed Soleil as unimportant only because of his little girl. Logically, I knew that. He wasn't unfeeling. Evanne just took precedence, and I could hardly fault him for that.

Except logic did nothing to relieve me of the all-too-familiar cold indifference that came with dismissal. No matter the explanations behind it, I knew what it was. I'd spent my entire life having it directed at me for one reason or another. Some understandable. Some not. All bullshit when it came down to it because neither side could truly understand what it meant to be the other one.

I would never know what it was like to have a family looking out for me, putting me first, being concerned with my well-being. Alec would never know what it was like to not have family. Even if he lost power and money, nothing short of being a horrible person would cause his family to walk away from him, and even then, I wasn't so sure.

When I climbed on the bus, I put all that behind me. I wouldn't do to Soleil what Alec had done. I wouldn't make my personal life take precedence over her safety. I could do what he could not. I could make *her* the important one.

And the way it started was by me going to the abandoned bowling alley that kids sometimes used when they needed a night away...or a place to meet someone they weren't supposed to be meeting. I was hoping the former was all there was to this.

THREE
ALEC

"ANSWER THE FUCKING PHONE!" I HUNG UP BEFORE I shouted the words, having enough presence of mind to want to keep Evanne from possibly hearing me yell.

It had been two hours since I'd gotten Keli's text, and I'd been waiting at the house the entire time, continuing to call and text but getting no response.

In all honesty, I had expected her to show up at some point, perhaps making me wait a while simply to see me squirm. Perhaps she intended to use this as a way to 'convince' me to rethink my decisions regarding custody of Evanne and my relationship with Lumen.

If that was her goal, she would be sorely disappointed. If anything, this proved that I could no longer trust Keli to do what was best for our child. For some reason, the rational woman who had cared so well for our daughter the first eight years of her life was gone. I suspected it was a combination of Alessandro having broken things off with Keli and then me deciding that I wanted to be with a woman other than her, but none of that excused Keli's actions.

"Fuck this." I grabbed my keys and jacket. I had given her time to come back without bringing the authorities into it. She had no one to blame but herself for the police getting involved.

The young man at the station's front desk looked barely old enough to be out of high school, much less wearing a police uniform. "Can I help you?"

"My ex-girlfriend took our daughter."

His jaw dropped open a little, and his eyes went wide. "W-what?"

I clenched my teeth and told myself I'd been abrupt. "I need to file a missing child report. My ex-girlfriend kidnapped our daughter."

"I...um..." He looked around, and I could see the panic in his eyes.

"Shite, man! Get a supervisor down here if you don't ken what yer about!" I slammed my hand on the counter.

"Is there a problem, Officer Baker?" A middle-aged woman in a uniform came over.

I met her halfway. "I have a child to report missing. Are you able to do that, or do I need to speak to someone else?"

"I can help you, Mr...?"

"McCrae," I snapped. "Alec McCrae."

Judging by the way the female officer's eyes widened, she recognized my name. For the first time in my life, I was prepared to use who I was to get something done.

"Come with me." The woman gestured for me to follow her. "We can speak in my office."

I followed her, tension vibrating through every cell in my body. I didn't want to sit, but when she stepped around behind her desk, intuition told me that she would be less likely to misinterpret my anger at Keli as being agitation in general. If a wealthy man of my build and height accused a woman of something, turning the suspicion toward myself would be far too easy. I needed them to keep the focus in the correct place.

As much as it pained me, I sat and tried to pretend that I wasn't teeming with impatience.

"Why don't you start from the beginning and tell me what's going on."

The beginning. *Shite*.

"My ex-girlfriend, Keli Miller, and I have an eight-year-old daughter, Evanne. Up until recently, Keli had primary custody, and I had visitations. At the end of August, Keli dropped Evanne off at my house with papers signing over primary custody to me because she was moving to Italy with her then-boyfriend. After the shooting at Kurt Wright where Evanne is a student, Keli returned. Since then, we have been trying to decide what would be best for our daughter, including a possibility of a reconciliation between us."

I stopped and waited while the officer finished jotting down some notes. When she was finished, she glanced up at me. "Go on."

I took a deep breath. "Last night, I told Keli that we would discuss drawing up a new custody agreement but that she and I would not be resuming a romantic relationship. She agreed and stated that she would take Evanne to school this morning due to my having a meeting. Except when I went to the school to pick up my daughter, Evanne wasn't there. Her teacher informed me that Keli had called Evanne in sick. While I was still speaking with Ms. Browne, I received a text from Keli."

I took out my phone and opened the messages. I held it out and then fell silent while she read, my fingers tapping on my knee.

Her face was unreadable as she handed my phone

back, but that was enough to tell me that she wouldn't be saying what I wanted her to say.

"You referred to her as your ex-girlfriend. The two of you were never married?"

I shook my head. "No."

"Is your name on Evanne's birth certificate as her father?"

"Yes." I gritted my teeth. She needed to know these things. "When Keli first told me she was pregnant, I was advised by the McCrae family lawyer that, if I was unwilling to marry Keli, I needed to be sure my name was on Evanne's birth certificate and I should keep track of all financial support I provided. I have done everything I had been advised to do."

She considered my answer for a moment and then nodded. "Did you file the custody papers she gave you before she left?"

"I did."

"But the change was voluntary, correct? She wasn't found unfit by the courts?"

I shook my head. "But if I have primary custody, her taking Evanne without my permission is kidnapping, is it not?" I forced myself to keep my voice low. "I don't want Keli in trouble, but I want my daughter back."

"Did she have specific visitation listed in the custody agreement?"

"No, just that I have primary custody."

"Here's the problem, Mr. McCrae." She dropped her pencil onto the pad, and I couldn't help but think she was buying herself a little time before breaking some bad news to me. "Custody is...tricky. Unless there's proof of neglect or abuse on behalf of either parent, even a detailed custody agreement is only as good as someone is willing to go to court on it."

"Are you saying Keli can simply leave with my daughter?"

"No, but..." She straightened. "It's custodial interference, and you can file with family court."

This entire trip had been a waste of time.

"There's a lot I can't do," she continued, "but that doesn't mean you're powerless. My hands are tied in ways yours aren't. You have resources available to you, and I – unofficially – encourage you to use them."

I stared at her, unsure if I was hearing her correctly. It sounded as if she was telling me to go outside the law.

"Understand me, Mr. McCrae, I am not suggesting you do something violent or foolish. But then, you don't strike me as a violent or foolish man." She stood up. "You strike me as the sort of man who will make strategic, intelligent choices to achieve your end goal."

I couldn't mask the surprise that I felt at her declaration. She knew who I was, but she didn't know me personally. How could she know I was smart enough to know what to do to get my daughter back?

"Do you have a recent picture?" she asked. "Of either of them or both of them? I'd like to give my people faces to look for. I may not be able to put out an Amber Alert or get a judge to issue an arrest warrant, but I can have eyes looking for them as everyone's on their daily business."

If I'd been less worried and upset, my gratitude would've been greater, but as it was, I managed a *thank you* as I pulled up a picture of the two of them together from our time with my family. She used my phone to send the picture to herself before handing it back.

"If anything changes, let me know."

Her offer was genuine, but that wouldn't do anything for me right now. She was right. I needed to reach out.

I drove back home, more because I didn't have a specific place to go than any other reason. Perhaps Keli would do the right thing and realize that she was only hurting herself by keeping Evanne away from me. If she did, the house was where she'd go.

I didn't believe she would do that, just as I didn't believe she was still in Seattle. Where she went was unimportant. The McCrae, Carideo, and Gracen families had a reach that went far beyond the city in which I made my home.

I had calls to make.

I didn't want to alarm my family, but they had to know, firstly because they loved Evanne as much as I did, and secondly, because they would never forgive me if I didn't ask them to use what was theirs to find her.

Making the calls also served another purpose. It allowed me to talk out what had happened and gather suggestions about what to do and ideas for where Keli could have gone. I hadn't realized until after I'd answered their questions, however, just how little I knew about the life Keli had made after we'd broken up. A life that my daughter had shared for eight years.

I had listened to everything Evanne had said about school and her room and the fun things she'd done. I'd ignored anything to do with Keli. I hadn't wanted to know anything about her, and it was only now I realized what a monumental mistake that was.

Today had been full of those.

Today, however, wasn't the day to dwell on those mistakes. There'd be plenty of time for that later.

I spent the next few hours pacing, writing down possibilities, making calls.

I didn't simply need to *find* Keli and Evanne. Once they were found, I needed a plan in place to get Evanne home and keep her safe. I hadn't wanted to keep Keli from her, but Keli had proven that she couldn't be trusted. The situation needed to be handled rather than delayed any longer. Putting it off was what had led to this point in the first place.

The law firm that exclusively handled all of my family's personal and business matters had lacked a family law expert, but I'd been given a recommendation. Percival Scarpa. The man was not only a highly admired legal mind, but one with integrity. After explaining my situation to him, he agreed to take my case, and we spent over an hour talking.

When our conversation was over, I felt better about that part of things, but I still had no idea how to find Evanne or Keli. Hiring private investigators seemed like the right move, and I had more than enough money for it, but I knew that the wrong ones could do more damage than good. I couldn't risk making another mistake.

The sound of the front door opening caught my attention, and my heart leaped. Not many people knew the security codes. However, it wasn't Keli or Evanne that I found coming down the hall. Red hair and vivid green eyes. A scar on the left side of his face. A familiar face. And a welcomed one.

"Eoin."

He gave me one of those half-hug, half-handshake

things that we'd always done. "Finding my niece seems like a better use of my time than bumming around our parents' house, feeling sorry for myself."

I'd never been so happy to see my little brother in my life.

FOUR
LUMEN

I would've asked myself if today could go any worse, but I was scared of how the universe might respond.

Soleil was still missing, and I'd been out until well past midnight looking for her. I would have stayed later if I'd had anywhere else to look or if I'd gotten another lead, but I'd exhausted more than just myself. Not only had Soleil not been at any of the places I'd looked, but no one there had seen her. I hadn't even gotten the slightest hint that anyone was lying.

I showered after I'd gotten home, hoping that it'd be enough to relax me into the right frame of mind to sleep, but I'd still laid awake for most of the rest of the night, which meant when my alarm went off, I'd been just as tired as I had been when I'd gotten into bed.

Things just continued downhill from there.

I'd spilled coffee on my skirt and had to change, but my only clean skirt didn't match my blouse. By the time I finished changing, I'd had to practically run to the bus stop, and there hadn't been any seats available, which meant I'd had to try to carry all of my things under one arm while keeping the other locked around a pole that had something unidentifiable and sticky on it.

Vice Principal Cornelius Harvey had been waiting for me when I arrived, which had turned the need for me to wash my hands into a good thing because I'd been able to offer a legitimate excuse to rush to the ladies' room. By the time I'd gotten back, enough other teachers had been around that he'd had to keep his distance. It hadn't stopped him from making comments under his breath regarding his theories about why I looked so haggard, but I'd ignored him.

Then there was Alec. I hadn't heard from him since we'd parted ways yesterday afternoon, so I didn't know if his silence was out of anger toward me, concern for Evanne, or him dealing with the aftermath of what Keli had done. Or a combination of all three of those things.

A part of me had optimistic hope that Evanne would walk in for class, and I'd know at least one of the two girls I cared about was safe. Well, safer, anyway. I believed what I'd said to Alec about how Evanne was at least safe with Keli. Yes, there would be things that Alec and Keli would have to deal with because of how Keli had handled things, and Evanne might have some confusion and difficult emotions to deal with, but the odds of Soleil's disappearance ending with her safe and sound went down with every passing hour.

I held on to that hope for several minutes after the first bell rang, but Evanne's seat remained empty. A part of me wished that I could call Alec and ask if she was back and he'd just kept her home to recover from the ordeal, but even if I'd been able to step away from my class to make a personal call, I doubted he'd want to hear from me.

"Good morning." I greeted my students with a smile and focused on getting through the day.

Fortunately for me, my class had music halfway through the morning, and after I walked them down to the music room, I went back to my classroom for a bit of peace and quiet.

Except Harvey was waiting for me, the scowl on his face saying I'd somehow managed to do something that displeased him. Unsurprisingly, I couldn't muster the energy to care much.

"You have a visitor waiting for you in the staff room."

I frowned. "Um, okay." I turned to go back the way I came.

Unfortunately, he came with me.

"You really should keep your personal life out of the workplace."

"Who's the visitor?" I figured that was safer than a straight-up denial since I had no idea if the person was actually connected to my personal life. I suddenly wondered if it was Soleil, but before I could get too hopeful, Harvey answered my question.

Sort of.

"Some guy. I didn't get his name." He scowled. "Big guy. Red hair. Ugly scar on his face."

My eyes widened. "I have absolutely no idea who that could be."

I could think of exactly zero people in my life who fit that description.

"Maybe he was a former...client." He gave me a sideways look. "You probably didn't see much of his face."

I gritted my teeth and swallowed a retort. Ever since he'd learned that Real Life Bodywork was a massage parlor, he'd stepped up his harassment. Verbally, anyway. He, at least, kept his hands to himself. I could handle the not-so-subtle hints about what services I could provide him with and questions about what services I had provided to other men. If he touched me, however, the mood I was in right now, I might knock out a few teeth, job be damned.

When I stepped into the staff room, all thoughts of whether or not I knew this guy flew out the window because I was staring at the scariest looking man I'd seen in a long time. A lean six-and-a-half-foot frame that looked strangely familiar. And a scar that ran from his temple to just under his mouth.

Shit.

"Um...hi?"

"Are you Lumen Browne?" His voice was as rough as his appearance.

"Yes." I still had no idea who he was or why he was here.

"Teacher to Evanne McCrae?"

I stiffened. "I don't talk about my students, especially with random strangers who come into my workplace asking questions."

One corner of his mouth quirked up in what might have been a smile at one time but seemed like it couldn't quite make it all the way. "I'm Eoin McCrae."

"Oh."

"I'm assuming that means you know who I am."

I had no idea how much he knew about Alec and me, and this wasn't the place or time to have that type of discussion. "I can hazard a guess that you're Evanne's uncle."

After a momentary pause, he nodded. "I'm helping my brother, and I need to ask you some questions about the last time you saw Evanne and what the usual procedures are for calling a child off sick."

"Of course." I sat down. "Anything I can do to help."

FIVE
ALEC

"THANK YOU. I APPRECIATE YOU CHECKING FOR ME."
I closed my eyes as I ended the call and reminded myself yet again that I shouldn't throw my phone. All that would do would lead to the hassle of having to purchase a new one.

I'd spent the entire morning calling hospitals and hotels, starting in Seattle and working my way out. Because I had no other ideas. None. Hospitals and hotels were the only two places I could think that I could check from home, and Eoin had made it perfectly clear that I wasn't to go anywhere. He was here to help, and I was supposed to stay here in case Keli and Evanne came back.

But I couldn't just sit here and do nothing. I could have worked from home, but how was I supposed to concentrate on anything if I didn't know where Evanne was?

I'd made more than two dozen calls, and not a single one of them turned up anything. For the hospitals, that was a good thing. I couldn't regret not finding them in a hospital. Not even Keli. As pissed as I was at her, I didn't want her hurt. I would have liked to find them at a hotel. I could have called Eoin, and we could have gone to get Evanne back. Problem solved.

But it wasn't as if I'd actually expected to find them. Keli was smart enough that if she really wanted to hide, she'd be far away from Seattle. I just had to hope that she hadn't prepared for what she'd done. If she had, she could have texted me from an airport and then disappeared into a random country with no way to track her.

Just the thought of it was enough to make me ill.

The front door opened again, but I didn't bother letting my hopes go anywhere. I expected Eoin back from wherever he'd gone, except it wasn't Eoin who came into the front room. It was another of my brothers. Brody was only two years younger than me, and it was thanks to him that I'd met Lumen.

The pain that came with her name was enough to make me wince, but not enough to make me forget our fight. Fortunately, Brody would help me forget it and get refocused on what was important.

"Brother." He went in for a real hug, smacking my back hard enough to sting. "You've got the worst fucking luck with women."

"Aye, I ken it well." I took a step back. "Do none of you ever call ahead?"

Brody smiled, blue-green eyes sparkling. "I'll take that to mean Eoin's already here."

"He is."

Brody looked around. "And he's...?"

"I have no idea," I said honestly. "He said he had to talk to some people."

"What does that mean?" Brody and I walked back to the living room and sat down.

"I have no idea," I said again. "I find that I often don't ken what that lad is up to."

"Me either," Brody admitted. "Once we get this squared away with Evanne and Keli, we should spend some time with him. I don't think he's doing as well as he wants us to think."

I nodded. I didn't like that I felt as if I was prioritizing my daughter over helping my brother. Logically, it made sense for me to put Evanne first. She was my daughter. She was missing. I needed to find her. Eoin was clearly functioning, and he was an adult.

But I kept hearing Lumen's voice in my head, asking me if Evanne was safe with Keli. Was it possible that my urgency in finding Evanne was causing me to overlook things that I should be seeing?

Brody kept my thoughts from wandering too far down that path as he brought me back to why he was there. "Have you thought of any other places they could be?"

"Not really," I said with a sigh. "I don't think they're in the area anymore, and I can't think of anything else."

"What about her parents? Where do they live?"

Shame flooded me. "I dinnae ken."

How could I not know where Keli's parents lived? How could I know so little about that part of my daughter's life?

"I'm a shite father," I muttered as I buried my face in my hands.

"You're not a shite father," Brody countered.

I raised my head. "My daughter is missing, and I can do fuck-all about it because I never bothered to find out anything about her mother other than the fact that she blames me for her art career not taking off."

Brody put his hand on my shoulder. "Aye, you've made mistakes, but that doesna make you a bad person. Just a human one."

"As opposed to a non-human person?" I asked dryly.

He grinned at me. "Now you're getting it."

After a moment of silence, I said, "Thank you for coming."

"Of course," he said, tone serious once more. "Back to Evanne, or rather, Keli. What do you remember her saying about her family? Anything could be helpful."

I thought back over the last nine years, trying to recall any conversation or hint where Keli's family had been mentioned.

"She grew up in Monterey Bay," I said finally. "Only child, so she has no siblings to take her in."

"Do her parents still live there?"

I shook my head. "I remember her saying something about her parents moving after she came to Seattle."

"Did she and Evanne ever visit them for holidays?"

"I don't believe so. They're not estranged because I know they've sent Evanne gifts for her birthday and Christmas, but I only met them shortly after Evanne was born. I don't think they live on the West Coast."

"So far enough away that travel is problematic, either because of cost or distance, or both?"

"That sounds about right." I frowned as a new thought occurred to me. "Keli didn't include any provisions for grandparent visitations in the documents she had drawn up before she went to Italy."

Brody ran his hand through his sandy brown hair. "Maybe they didn't agree with her moving to another country. They mighta been pissed at her for leaving their granddaughter in Seattle with you instead of with them. Could that have played a role in Keli taking Evanne? Trying to get back into her parents' good graces?"

"Possibly." But that didn't feel quite right either. "If that's the case, that would be the place she'd go."

He nodded his agreement.

Before either of us could explore the idea further, Eoin came inside. He and Brody greeted each other, but I didn't bother getting up. We would end up sitting in here anyway. It seemed like a waste of energy better spent elsewhere.

"Where have you been?" The question came out far harsher than I'd intended. "Sorry. That wasn't how I meant it."

"Don't worry about it." Eoin made a dismissive gesture as he came over to sit across from me. "It's not as if you don't have anything stressful going on at the moment."

Brody returned to sitting on the sofa next to me. "All right, what did you find?"

"I went to Evanne's school and spoke with her teacher."

"You did what?" This time, I wouldn't apologize for my tone. Not when Eoin had gone poking his nose into a part of my personal life that had no bearing on where Evanne was right now.

"I needed to know some procedural things, as well as whether or not Evanne had said anything that could have indicated Keli planning this for a while." Eoin's voice was mild, as if I hadn't tried to bite his head off. "If this wasn't a spur-of-the-moment decision, it's possible Keli might have said something to Evanne, who later repeated it to a teacher. Keli might think to tell Evanne not to say anything to you, but it's doubtful she would've thought the same of teachers."

"Unless Keli knew that Evanne's teacher was more than a teacher," Brody said.

I glared at him. "Aye, Keli knew that Lumen and I had been seeing each other, but that's no longer an issue."

Both brothers gave me nearly identical expectant looks.

"It has nothing to do with finding Evanne, and that's what's important," I reminded them.

"Aye, all right." Brody held up a hand. "What did you learn, Eoin?"

"Evanne didn't mention anything about going anywhere with her mother, and from what Lumen said about how much Evanne shares with her, that most likely means Keli didn't plan this."

Hope had my heart rate leaping. "That's good, right?"

"I think so," Eoin agreed. "That means she most likely didn't have passports and plane tickets already purchased. No money stashed or go bags."

My brother's logic eased some of my tension. "Which means she's still in the US."

"Not a small bit of ground to search," Brody said, "but a far sight better than trying to find her in other countries."

"We need to know what resources she has available." Eoin leaned forward and grabbed a pen and paper. "Alec, you're going to look into that since you have access to financial records, that sort of thing. Talk to your accountant, your money manager, whoever's involved with the money you give to Keli and Evanne. Find out if they know about other accounts Keli might have, other sources of income. Debt. Credit cards. Cash. Jewelry. Anything she could use to fund this."

I nodded, impressed with Eoin's handling of the situation. When he'd said he'd come to help, I hadn't expected this level of professionalism.

"Brody, you're going to handle the social media aspect of things. Any accounts Keli or Evanne have, get into them. Go through Keli's friends and followers. See if she contacted anyone before she ran. Make a list of people who seemed like they'd be willing to hide Keli if she needed it. Focus on men who might be trying to get in good with Keli and on women who came from situations where they wanted or did escape from ex-boyfriends and ex-husbands."

Judging by the surprise on Brody's face, he hadn't been expecting this from Eoin either. I had no doubt that Brody was also thinking that perhaps what had happened to Eoin wouldn't send him spiraling back down to where he'd been before he'd enlisted.

"I'm going to check out transportation. Airports, rental places, train stations, bus depots. I'll need some pictures of both Keli and Evanne to show around. If you have a family picture of me and Evanne, even if it's a group one, that'll help too. Prove I'm not some pervert searching for a little girl and just claiming to be her uncle."

"I have plenty of pictures on my phone and laptop." I started tapping at the keyboard. "I'll get several printed up."

"Good." Eoin leaned forward, his expression earnest. "Don't worry. We're going to find them, and Evanne will be fine."

For the first time since I'd realized Evanne was missing, I truly believed that things would be okay. We could do this. We could find Evanne and bring her home.

SIX
LUMEN

I MADE IT.

The last hour had been pushing it, my nerves stretched to the breaking point, my head pounding. Between the kids asking where Evanne was and Eoin's visit, my missing student had been on my mind, but so had Soleil since my check-in with Brie had resulted in learning absolutely nothing new.

What that meant was that, when I was thinking about one of them, I was feeling guilty about not thinking about the other. And when my attention was on my students, I felt like I should be worrying about one or the other...

Needless to say, by the time I stepped out into yet another dreary day, my head felt like it was going to explode. All I wanted to do was go home, take a long hot bath, and curl up in bed with a book.

But there were two missing girls, and I had to find at least one of them. I wouldn't be able to sleep or relax or do anything but worry and feel sick until they were both safe and sound. Alec probably had half the state looking for Evanne. I would work on Soleil.

I called Josalyn while I rode the bus to the group home.

"Any news?" I asked.

"Not yet," she said with a sigh. "But I was able to file a missing person report finally. I don't know how much good it'll do, but it's there, at least."

I didn't need to ask why she thought filing a police report wouldn't help much. No matter how much the authorities wanted to be able to follow every lead on every missing person report, they just didn't have the manpower to do it. Unfortunately, a fourteen-year-old foster kid fell into the 'most likely a runaway' category, which meant it would be a lower priority than, say, a missing person with evidence of foul play.

"And no one's heard from her?"

"Not that I know of."

I rubbed my forehead. "All right. I'm heading over to the house now. I'll let you know if Brie's heard anything."

"Be careful, Lumen," Josalyn said.

"I will," I promised before ending the call. I meant it, but I wasn't going to change my plans to go search for Soleil. I'd do it as carefully as I could, but I wouldn't hide in my apartment simply because it was dangerous.

I spent the rest of the ride marking up homework in the hope that I'd have less to do after I got home tonight. I managed to finish a few minutes before my stop, cramming the papers back into my bag in time to be on my feet when the door opened. The rain had turned to a nasty sort of slush, and even my umbrella couldn't keep it from soaking into my slacks as I walked.

This was going to be miserable.

"Lumen!" Diana charged at me the moment I stepped inside the house.

I barely got my arms open before she wrapped her arms around my waist and squeezed. "Good to see you."

"Will you find Soleil?" Her big eyes shown with unshed tears. "She hasn't been home in days, and I miss her even though she could be mean to me sometimes. Can you help me with my homework? Kaitlyn is supposed to do that today but she–"

"All right, Diana." Brie appeared and eased Diana away from me. "Why don't you go get started on your homework while Lumen and I talk?"

To my surprise, Diana did as she was told without

arguing. I called out greetings to the other kids as I followed Brie through the living room and into the kitchen. A couple of the kids shouted back, but a couple completely ignored me. No surprises there.

Brie wiped her forehead with the back of her hand. "Can I get you something to drink?"

I shook my head. "No, thank you. I just wanted to touch base about Soleil."

"Have you talked to Josalyn?" Brie took a bottle of juice from the fridge and then leaned against the counter.

"She said she filed a report." The expression on Brie's face said she knew what that meant as well as I did. I blew out a long breath. "It's always possible a cop will run into her at some point."

"That would be something," Brie said, pressing the cold bottle against her cheek, "but we both know that if the cops find her, it'll probably be because she's gotten in trouble."

She was right. Unfortunately. The longer Soleil was missing, the more likely it was that she'd end up in juvie or worse...and that was if she was ever found at all.

"So, none of the kids have heard from her? No feeling that they're lying?"

Brie shrugged. "My gut says no. Soleil keeps to herself."

"Have you thought of any other things she might've said that could give me an idea where to look? I'll go back to the places I went last night too, just in case she shows up there, but I'd like to have some new options."

"Her grandmother passed last year, and that was the only family she had left." Brie rolled the bottle between her hands. "She used to spend time there. Maybe she went back? Wanted to see the place for old times' sake?"

"Possibly," I agreed. I doubted it, but I was willing to try anything. "Do you have an address?"

"Let me check her file."

Twenty minutes later, I was leaving with a single new lead and still-damp shoes. I meant what I'd said about checking out the same places I had before, but now I was hoping that wouldn't be necessary. Perhaps she'd made friends living near her grandmother and had wanted to go see them.

Maybe I was being naïve, but I was trying to lean toward optimistic.

I took the train this time to keep me from walking between bus stops. Plus, the seats were much more comfortable and the time shorter. I was willing to spend a little extra to have that.

The walk from the train station to the apartment building wasn't a long one, but it was a wet one. For a

Seattle native, that wasn't really anything new, but that didn't mean I liked it.

The grandmother had lived on the third floor, which made that my first stop. Apartment by apartment, I knocked on doors and smiled at people who looked less than pleased to see a stranger who wanted to ask questions about a missing kid. Some of them recognized her, but only from back when Soleil had spent time with her grandmother. No one had seen her since then.

Two hours, and all her work led to was a dead end.

Wonderful.

By the time I made it back down to the lobby, I realized I actually did have more than one new lead because there were places around here that I wouldn't have checked before learning that Soleil had spent time in this neighborhood. I didn't have any specific places in mind, but I did know a little about Soleil. I was confident I could guess a few places she might've gone if she'd come back here.

I stood at the door for a couple minutes to get my bearings, then headed out. I went the opposite way as the train station, wishing I'd gone home long enough to drop off my bag. It hadn't seemed that heavy when I'd left the school, but now, it was getting annoying. By the end of the night, my shoulder would be aching.

Still, I had no plans to give up. I had places to check. A late-night deli. A mini-mart. Two liquor stores.

I saw a few places where groups of teens and young adults were gathered, talking, and smoking. I got some funny looks when I came up to them and asked about Soleil, but they didn't seem evasive when they said they hadn't seen her.

I'd intended to go back to the places I'd checked last night, but by the time I walked up one side, then back down to where the train station was, I knew I had to go home. If I ran myself down too much, I wouldn't be any good to anyone.

I called Brie on the way back home and told her that I hadn't found anything. She wasn't surprised, and if I was being totally honest, I wasn't either. The longer Soleil was gone, the more I believed that her reason for leaving was somehow connected to the strange phone call she'd made to me on the day of the shooting.

I was still puzzling over it when I arrived home. Mai had texted me a couple hours ago to say she wouldn't be home until around two or three, so I planned to shower and crawl straight into bed.

The moment I stepped into the hallway, however, everything changed.

There, huddled on the floor next to my door, was a

battered and bloody body, barely conscious, but awake enough to croak my name.

Soleil.

SEVEN

LUMEN

I NEEDED TO GET A FUCKING CAR!

"For the third time, I don't know what happened!" I practically shouted at the phone. I'd set it on the floor after dialing 911, and now it was on speaker, so I didn't really need to yell, but the operator was pissing me off.

Fortunately, she was good enough at her job that she wasn't taking offense. She was clearly used to desperate, terrified people.

"Is she still conscious?"

"Soleil? Soleil, it's Lumen." I wanted to shake her or touch her face or do something that would give me a better idea of how aware she was, but she looked so horrible that I didn't think it was a good idea to do any of that. What if she had internal bleeding, and I made it worse? "I think her eyes are open, but she's not responding to anything I say. Her face is so swollen, I can't tell for sure."

"Okay. Keep talking to her. Give her something to focus on."

The sound of sirens sent a rush of relief through me. "The ambulance is here."

"All right. I'm going to let you go, okay?"

"Yes, yes. Thank you." I ended the call and shoved my phone back in my purse. "It's going to be okay, Soleil. Paramedics are coming. We'll get you to the hospital, and you'll be okay. We'll find out who did this to you."

Through the puffy flesh surrounding her eyes, I caught a sliver of color, as if she was trying to focus on my face. Her hand reached for me, lips moving without any sound.

"I'm right here," I reassured her. "I'm right here, and I'm not going anywhere."

I heard footsteps coming up the stairs, but I didn't look away. Knowing I had to be strong for her kept me from breaking down...or doing something stupid. At the moment, concern was strongest, but grief and anger simmered below the surface, and I knew that as soon as I let them loose, I would need an outlet, even if that outlet was screaming and crying in my shower.

I couldn't do that here. Soleil needed me to be strong and calm. Besides, if I was freaking out, someone would have to take their attention from the girl to work on me. Those thoughts kept my emotions boxed up tight and allowed me to have enough common sense to move out of the way when the paramedics arrived. I didn't go far, though.

"Her name's Soleil Artz," I said before either man could ask. "She's a foster kid and has been missing for the last two days. I was out looking for her, and when I got home about ten minutes ago, I found her like this. She said my name, but that's it."

"She's your foster kid?" the older of the two men asked as he examined her.

"No, more like a little sister. Sort of." I shook my head. "She's in the same foster home where I grew up, and I volunteer there. I've been trying to help her."

"How old is she?" the other paramedic asked as he pulled out a clipboard.

"Fourteen."

The older one glanced up. "Do you have contact information for her legal guardian?"

"I do." I reached for my bag. "I have her case worker's number too. Should I call them both?"

With something to focus on, I was able to give the paramedics as much information as I had, and by the time I finished, I was in the ambulance with them and on the way to the hospital. After confirming that it'd be okay to make a couple calls, I reached out to Brie first. She didn't answer.

"Hey, Brie, it's Lumen. I'm with Soleil on my way to the hospital. She showed up at my place beaten up pretty badly. I'll call Josalyn too. I'll stay at the hospital until you get there." I double-checked the hospital name and gave that as well before hanging up. I then tapped Josalyn's name. She answered on the second ring, and I repeated pretty much everything I'd just said. After muttering a few choice expletives, she said she'd meet me there.

With that done, I put my phone away and focused on holding Soleil's hand and telling her that she was going to be okay.

I hoped that, at some point, I'd start to believe it too.

SIX. Seven. Eight.

Turn.

One. Two. Three...

I counted each step with deliberation, as if focusing on a number, a place to turn and start walking again, would keep me from wondering and worrying about what was happening in the back.

Because I'd come in with her and was able to answer

a few questions, I'd gotten more information than I probably would've if I'd come in separately, but I knew they would probably give me the 'sorry, you're not family' line from here on out. I understood it, and I agreed with needing laws to protect patients' privacy. It just made situations like this, where family didn't necessarily mean *family*, more difficult.

"Lumen, thank you for staying."

I turned to see Josalyn hurrying toward me, heels clicking on the linoleum. "They took her straight back, and I haven't heard anything since."

"Did she say what happened?"

I shook my head, shifting my weight from one foot to the other. "She said my name when I first saw her, but after that, not a word." I shivered, suddenly all too aware that my clothes were wet and clammy. "It looked really bad. Blood everywhere. Clothes torn. She looks like someone beat the shit out of her."

Josalyn's mouth flattened into a line. "Fuck."

"That pretty much sums it up, yeah," I said dryly.

She didn't say anything for a minute, those intelligent eyes studying me. Then, finally, "Do you want to wait with me until we find out what's what?"

I rolled my neck, hoping to relieve a bit of the tension. "I told her I wouldn't leave her."

"Excuse me." A tired-looking woman in green scrubs

came into the waiting room. "You're the one who came in with the girl a while ago, right? Are you family?"

"She doesn't have family," Josalyn said. "Soleil Artz is a ward of the state. I'm her caseworker, Josalyn Brodie. This is Lumen Browne, the young lady who found Soleil."

"Are there foster parents?"

"A foster mom," Josalyn said. "We're still trying to get ahold of her. For now, you can speak to me." The doctor glanced at me. "It's all right. She can hear it too."

The doctor nodded and then gestured at the chairs. "We should sit."

My stomach fell. Shit. The doctor's face was expressionless as the three of us sat down, and that scared me. The worse things were, the more people tried to pretend they weren't reacting at all.

"Miss Artz has multiple lacerations and contusions," the doctor began, "all consistent with being beaten, most likely with fists. A few of the injuries could have been caused by a leather strap, possibly a belt."

My nails dug into my palms.

"Four of her ribs are broken. The zygomatic bone on the left side is cracked in two places." The doctor touched the side of her face to show us what she meant. "Two of her fingers are fractured. Her wrists and ankles are rubbed almost completely raw, as if she'd been bound."

My stomach lurched, and I pressed my lips together. I didn't want to hear the rest, but I had to. If I was going to help Soleil through this, I had to know it all.

"She wouldn't tell us what happened," the doctor continued, "but she did consent to a rape exam, mostly, I think, because she knew she needed medical attention."

Fuck.

"She was raped." Josalyn made it a statement rather than a question.

"She didn't say it, but the evidence is there, yes." The lines around the doctor's eyes tightened. "I believe by more than one man."

"Fuck." My hand went over my mouth.

"I gave her something for the pain, so she's resting now. The police will want to talk to her, but I'm not sure they'll get much more out of her than I did." She stood. "I'm not sure how long I want to keep her yet. A lot will depend on how some of the test results come back."

She didn't say what those tests were for, but considering what had happened to Soleil, it wasn't difficult to figure out. STD tests. The kind of animals who would rape and beat up a fourteen-year-old kid wouldn't give a shit about passing something along. Whether or not they thought about leaving DNA was a mixed blessing. Condoms meant no semen, but also a lower likelihood of pregnancy or disease.

"Will she be out for the night?" Josalyn asked.

"Most likely. That's what I'll tell the police when they show up anyway. Kid needs her rest."

"Good." Josalyn stood up. "If you could let them know that I'll be back when visiting hours start, they can talk to her then, if she's up to it."

I almost asked where she was going, but that was a stupid question. Soleil wasn't Josalyn's only case. She'd have to be up tomorrow for work, and a lot of that was going to be paperwork for this. She couldn't spend the entire night here while Soleil slept.

"Would I be allowed to stay with her?" I asked. "I don't want her to wake up and see I'm not there after I promised her that I wouldn't leave her."

The doctor looked at Josalyn, who nodded. "I think that can be arranged."

"Good. Um, I just need to call my roommate. I don't want her to worry when she gets home, and I'm not there."

"You do that, and I'll have someone put a chair in there for you."

"Thank you. I'll be back in a couple minutes." I went with Josalyn to the lobby, waving as she kept going out to her car. It was well past one in the morning, but I called Mai anyway.

"What's wrong?"

A lump formed in my throat at the concern in my friend's voice. When this was over, I'd make sure Mai knew just how grateful I was to have her. If I was ever hurt or sick, I'd never have to worry about going through it alone. I always had Mai.

"Soleil's in the hospital." The words came out in a rush. "She was at the apartment when I got home, and someone beat her up...probably more than one someone. They... some...they..." My voice broke. "*Shit*."

"It's okay." Mai's voice was gentle. "You don't have to say it."

I cleared my throat. "I'm going to stay the night. I don't want her to be here alone."

"Do you want me to come there?"

I loved that she offered. "No, I think the fewer people, the better. She's going to have to talk to the cops tomorrow as it is."

"Damn."

"Yeah." A moment of silence passed. "I'm going to go now."

"If you need me, say the word. Love you."

"You too."

As I hung up the phone, I stared at the screen, filled

with a sudden urge to call Alec. To hear his voice. The need was so intense it was almost painful, but it wasn't the right thing to do. He had Keli and Evanne to deal with. And he'd made it perfectly clear that's where his priorities were. Rightfully so.

I just didn't know if I could handle that rejection again.

Better to not even try.

EIGHT

ALEC

"The number you are trying to reach is no longer a working number. Please hang up and try the call again."

"Fuck!!" I threw my phone at the couch and watched it bounce off the cushion and onto the carpet. If I'd had worse aim, buying a new mobile would've been my next action.

Keli had disconnected her phone.

She was one of those people who always needed her phone, which meant that this was more serious than I'd hoped. If she'd simply taken off, panicked, overreacted, that was one thing. Canceling her phone was something else entirely. She had crossed from something she could explain away to making a deliberate choice to prevent me from even talking to my daughter.

How could I have missed this? Why hadn't I seen the desperation Keli must have felt to do something this drastic? Had there been no signs? Or had I just been too enamored with Lumen to see what was happening right in front of me?

My phone rang, and I snatched it up, unable to stop myself from hoping it would be good news. When I saw *Da* on the screen, the hope died, replaced by the urgent need to talk to my father.

"Morning, Da."

"Nothing new?"

The familiar rumble in that thick accent took me back to when a word from my father had still been enough to make me know all was right with the world. No matter how old I was, I believed there would always be times when I needed him. Having lost one parent young, I had vowed I would always appreciate having Da still here. Today, more than any other day in a long time, I was grateful for his presence.

"Her phone's been disconnected."

"Shite."

"Aye." I sighed and closed my eyes as I dropped down onto the couch. "I thought for sure it'd be over by now. A day or two and Keli would come to her senses."

"Instead, she's making it harder to find her and

Evanne," he said. "Deliberate decisions that cannae be explained away by panic."

"Exactly." I let a minute of silence stand between us before speaking again. "Is this my fault? Did I miss seeing this coming?"

"No, lad. This isn't on you. Keli is the one in the wrong here. And none of us could have guessed she'd do this."

"How annoyed is Theresa?" I pressed my palm over my eyes. "The whole point of me taking over as the CEO of MIRI was to let you enjoy your retirement in peace, and here I am dragging you back in."

"I've had twelve years of watching you build our family's company beyond anything I could have hoped for. It's not too much for me to step back up when you need me."

I coughed to clear my throat. "That doesna answer my question."

"MIRI is the last thing on her mind, lad. She and Paris are working on Missing Persons posters and scouring social media for any sign of Keli or Evanne. The only reason I was able to get them to stay here was reminding them that we would be the second most likely place Evanne would go if she got away."

"I hadn't thought of that," I admitted. "I feel as if there should be so much more I'm doing."

"You cannae think of everything."

Logically, I knew that was true, but logic didn't always win out in these situations.

"Which brings me to the second reason for my call." I listened to him inhale deeply. "What do you think about going public? Issuing a press release to appeal not only to the public to watch for Evanne, but to Keli herself, to ask her to bring Evanne home?"

"I'm torn about it," I said honestly. "I want to believe that the more people looking, the better the likelihood of finding them, but another part of me is worried about what it would do to Evanne if she saw her family saying negative things about her mother."

Da sighed. "Aye, I thought that too."

"I'll ask Eoin what he thinks. He seems to have a good head for this sort of thing."

"Aye, he does."

"Tell Mom and Paris thank you," I said. "And can you pass along things to everyone else? I donnae have the energy to talk to that many people right now."

"Aye, lad. Of course."

"Thanks, Da."

After a few seconds of silence, the call ended, and I dropped the phone next to me. I put my head back, closing my eyes and wishing that this was all a nightmare. I wasn't usually one to entertain such fanciful ideas, but I was at my wits' end, without an idea of what to do or where to go next.

"Alec."

I turned my head as Eoin came into the living room. "Aye?"

"You've been talking to Da." Without waiting for an answer, Eoin came over to sit on the edge of the chair closest to the couch. "I just got a call."

I sat up straight. "From?"

"Vice Principal Cornelius Harvey from Kurt Wright School."

"Bastard."

Eoin's eyebrows went up. "I'm assuming you're not a fan?"

I growled, and my brother's eyebrows rose even further. "He's one of those arseholes who think his position means he can do or say whatever he wishes, and no one can stop him."

Eoin frowned. "Is he an honest arsehole?"

I shrugged. "I doubt it. Our few interactions make me think he's the type of man who will twist things until they suit his needs."

"All right, then, I suppose any information I get from him needs to come with a grain of salt."

"What information?" I asked, leaning forward, my elbows on my knees.

"Evanne's teacher wasn't at work today."

"I don't understand why that's pertinent. When she chooses to take days off is none of my business." I tried not to think about who Lumen might be spending the day with.

"Alec, come on. You're involved with this woman, and that's when Keli decides to take off with Evanne? She isn't around, helping us look, and then she calls off? You have to admit, it looks suspicious."

I stared at him. "You think Lumen is involved with Keli and Evanne's disappearance?"

He lifted his hands, palms up. "I'm saying it looks bad is all."

"No." I shook my head. "Lumen has things going on in her own life. That's why she hasn't been here helping us look for Evanne."

Not to mention the shitty way I'd treated her, no matter how justified I felt at my anger.

"Besides, she'd have no motive."

"Money's always a motive," Eoin said quietly. "Maybe Keli paid her."

I thought of the financial information I'd uncovered. Keli would have had the resources. But, still, I couldn't believe it.

"Not Lumen. She'd never do something like that to

Evanne. There's another explanation about where she is today."

"You've heard from her, then?"

"No, but it's not possible."

"What's not possible?" Brody joined us, the bags under his eyes telling me he'd gotten as little sleep as the rest of us.

"Lumen having a hand in this," I said. "It's a non-issue." When Eoin opened his mouth, I held up a hand. "We have other matters to discuss. First, Keli canceled her phone."

"Shit," Eoin said.

"My thought exactly. And I just spoke with Da. He said Theresa and Paris want to do a press release to appeal to the public. I wasn't sure how good of an idea that would be."

"I agree," Eoin said. "I think the benefits might outweigh the negatives. Let's compare everything we found yesterday and then decide whether or not Mom should say something."

"If you do, she's the best one for it," Brody said. "She can hold it together, but not look too unemotional."

Eoin nodded. "It may be time to go more on the offensive. What did you guys come up with yesterday?"

NINE

LUMEN

I was in a seriously shitty mood, and the way that things were going, it didn't look like it would be getting better any time soon.

Sleeping in the hospital chair had been nearly impossible, despite how thoroughly exhausted I'd been. And still was. Besides the fact that the chair was one of the most uncomfortable things I'd ever sat on, our surroundings weren't exactly quiet. I probably could've dealt with both of those things, however, if it hadn't been for the nurses coming in and out every hour or so to check on Soleil.

Then, around dawn, Soleil had woken up, agitated and thrashing around. I'd helped calm her down, assuring her that she was safe, and she wasn't alone. She'd managed to say something about how "she'd never be safe," but before I could get any additional information from her, she'd passed out.

While waiting for Soleil to wake up again, I'd finally gotten ahold of Brie. She'd had to take Lorelai – a special needs foster child with both mental and physical issues – to an emergency room on the other side of the city. Even though Lorelai was older than Soleil, her mentality was much younger, and she panicked when left alone in unfamiliar places. With Brie in an impossible position, I'd offered to stay with Soleil until Brie could either come or Soleil was discharged.

That had led to me having to call off from work. Alice had been polite about it, but I didn't have any illusions about how the faculty would take it, especially Cornelius Harvey. I'd have to deal with the fallout eventually, but at least that had been something I could put off until a future date. I had plenty on my plate to deal with right now anyway.

I'd just come back from getting a cup of the worst coffee I'd ever tasted when two people walked into Soleil's room. A pair of detectives had arrived to take her statement. Neither of them had been happy when I'd informed them that they'd need to wait until Josalyn arrived, but then Soleil had announced that it didn't matter if Josalyn was there or not. She wasn't going to say a word about what had happened.

I'd tried to convince her otherwise, promising that I'd make sure she was safe, but she'd simply turned her head and closed her eyes. The cops had been pissed, but I'd at least gotten the impression that their anger hadn't been directed at Soleil. They hadn't looked at her and seen a problem child who was wasting their time. They'd seen a victim too scared to make an accusation.

I'd followed them out and given them as much information as I'd been able, including Brie's and Josalyn's names, but I'd known that the chances of them finding out what'd happened with only that little bit of info was slim. I'd tried to tell Soleil that when I'd gone back into the room, but she'd still refused to say anything.

I'd hoped Josalyn would be able to convince her otherwise, but Soleil had refused to even look at either of us. A part of me wished she'd get angry or show some type of emotion when we pushed her, but she hadn't responded at all. Josalyn had tried for half an hour before needing to go back to work. She hadn't wanted to go, but I'd assured her that I'd stay.

And that was how I found myself currently sitting in Soleil's room, listening to a doctor patiently explaining for the third time why they were waiting for additional test results before releasing her.

"I don't give a shit about test results. I want to go."

Soleil had her arms crossed and what was probably

supposed to be a stubborn set to her jaw, but the swollen, discolored flesh of her face made her look more like the frightened child she was than the hardass she was trying to be.

"You're a minor, Miss Artz. You won't be discharged without a guardian present, and your caseworker left instructions for us to process all of the necessary blood-work before contacting your foster mom."

"Fuck that."

I stood and crossed over to the bed. "Soleil, the tests are already out. What will it hurt to wait? It's not like they need to draw more blood or anything."

"Why can't you people just leave me alone?"

The pain-filled undercurrent to that question made my heart hurt. "We're all trying to help you, and to do that, questions need to be answered."

Her pulse was throbbing in her neck. "If you gave a damn, you'd just leave me alone."

"No." I kept my voice low but firm. "Not about this. Your doctors need information to treat you. Just stay until those are done, and I'll call Brie myself."

"How long?"

"An hour, maybe two," the doctor answered.

"Look at it this way," I said. "Here, you get a room all to yourself and can watch whatever you want on TV without crazy kids running around."

Very slowly, I watched her soften. "All right. But nothing new."

I looked at the doctor, and he nodded. "Nothing new."

The doctor and nurse left, and I pulled my chair up next to the bed, angling it so I could see the television. I didn't particularly care what was on, but I knew if I acted like I'd moved closer to her so she would talk to me, she wouldn't say a word. It was better to let conversation happen naturally.

After a half hour, however, Soleil hadn't said a single word.

"We've all been looking for you," I said finally. "You scared the shit out of us."

"Didn't think anyone would notice," she muttered, not looking at me.

"Of course we noticed." I reined in my emotions and forced my words to remain even. The last thing she needed right now was to feel like I was attacking her. "We had no idea where you'd gone...or even if someone had taken you."

Maybe that wasn't as subtle as it should have been, but I at least hadn't flat-out asked her for additional details.

Her nostrils flared. "I can take care of myself."

I didn't point out the obvious. Soleil wasn't a stupid

kid. Arguing with her wouldn't do anything but close her off even more. Still, I couldn't just say nothing.

"When I was a kid, before I moved into Brie's house, I was in this one home with a boy named Toby. He was a teenager, so we didn't really talk much. One day, I saw him shoving some stuff in his backpack. He told me not to say anything, and he'd give me a present. I didn't know what to do. Before I had to figure it out, though, he got picked up for possession." I shifted in my chair, trying to find a more comfortable position. "Everybody tried to get Toby to turn on the guy who gave him the drugs. He wouldn't do it. While he was with the cops, one of the other kids got into some drugs Toby still had hidden in his room. Welby. He was six, and his body just couldn't handle it. Toby still refused to tell anyone why he was selling or who he was selling to. He got sixteen years but didn't make it four. They didn't trust him to not talk."

Anger and something closer to fear flashed in the girl's eyes. "What, so I don't snitch, and I'm gonna die? That what you're saying?"

I shook my head. "Just saying that sometimes, it's worth it to take a risk and trust someone."

Maybe, one day, she'd get it.

TEN

ALEC

Eoin's name popped up on my phone screen, and I turned away from my computer as I answered.

"Hello."

"I have something," Eoin said instead of a greeting. "I'm at a car rental place in Bellevue, and the clerk recognized Keli. She was in here Wednesday afternoon with Evanne."

Shit. He'd done it. He'd gotten us a lead.

He kept going. "She used her real license to rent it, but that was before she canceled her phone number, so she might not be using it anymore."

"But she's in Bellevue? Or at least coming back to the rental place there?"

"Unfortunately, she chose an open-ended rental

agreement where she can turn in the car at a different location and at a time she chooses."

I scowled. "They must have some way of keeping track of the car."

"They have GPS, but we won't get that information without a court order." Eoin's frustration bled into his words. "They also won't tell me if the car has been turned in yet."

I closed my eyes and tried to rein in my disappointment. Eoin had found something. The fact that it wouldn't immediately lead to finding my daughter didn't lessen my gratitude. I had to make certain that I didn't take out my frustration on him.

"I know this isn't as good as it could have been," he said, "but I'll figure something out. I'm not giving up."

"It's not your fault," I said with a sigh. "If they won't release the information without a warrant or subpoena or whatever legal document they need, it's out of your hands."

"The fuck it is," he muttered. "If the manager hadn't come in when she did, I could've gotten the info out of the clerk no matter what their policy is."

I was half tempted to tell him to work on the clerk when the manager was gone, but Eoin wasn't an easy person to forget. If he continued to push the clerk, it could backfire not only against the clerk but against my brother. Unless I had reason to believe Evanne was in danger, I didn't want to risk Eoin getting into trouble. Not when I had other options.

"I'll talk to the police again," I said. "And I'll speak to Percival Scarpa first. Perhaps he'll have some ideas about how to get the information we need."

"I didn't think the cops could do anything."

"Maybe it'll be different now that there's proof she's actively avoiding me." I didn't know if I was simply grasping at straws or if that could indeed be the case, but I could hear helplessness in Eoin's voice. Helplessness that I also felt. If I could do anything to make him see that he was contributing even if he didn't necessarily feel like it, I would do it.

"I'm going to do some research into the rental place," Eoin said. "It's not a huge chain, which might mean there are only a few of them around. I'll start with the closest ones and work my way out. Hopefully, someone else will have seen her."

I didn't bother to tell him that sounded like something far too involved for a single person to do. I'd learned at a young age not to tell Eoin when he couldn't do something...unless I specifically wanted that thing done. With this, I decided I would support whatever he thought was best to do.

Besides, there was always the off chance that he

could find Keli and Evanne. I simply wasn't willing to bet everything on it. Not with the sort of luck I'd had recently.

After a few more minutes discussing possibilities, Eoin ended the call, and I went to get my car keys. If things went badly, a drive might be a good way to release some of this tension.

The same young man who had been at the desk before was there again. The expression on his face said he remembered me, and it wasn't a pleasant memory.

"Officer Baker," I said with a tight smile. "My daughter is still missing."

"One moment, Mr. McCrae. I'll get my supervisor."

At least he wasn't wasting any time.

Five minutes later, I was back in the same office across from the same woman as before. At least I wouldn't have to re-explain everything, just give her an update.

"My ex still hasn't returned our daughter," I began. "She's also canceled her phone line, leaving me unable to even leave voicemails or send text messages to my daughter."

The officer frowned. "That does present a problem."

"And I've recently learned that Keli rented a car from a rental place in Bellevue and arranged to drop it off at another place. The cars have GPS, but I don't have access to that information. Not without...legal inter-vention."

"Which is why you're here again." She made it a statement rather than a question.

"It is." I folded my arms. "Now, what are the chances you'll actually be doing something to help me?"

"Unfortunately, Mr. McCrae, this is still a matter for family court. A custody issue, not a criminal matter." She leaned forward, putting her elbows on her desk. "This may not be a necessary piece of advice, but I'm going to give it to you anyway. Retain legal counsel. Make yourself too visible to ignore."

As much as I loathed the idea, it was one I had been contemplating myself. I had never liked the idea of using who I was or the money I had to receive special treat-ment. But, if that was the only way I could get Evanne back, I would do it. I would use everything I had, burn any bridge, storm any stronghold.

I would *not* be helpless.

ELEVEN
LUMEN

I'd never been this tired in my entire life.

Seriously.

I'd almost fallen asleep taking the elevator down to the hospital lobby after Brie arrived to take Soleil home. If the ride had been any longer, I might've given someone quite a shock, thinking I'd had a heart attack or something.

Soleil had barely even looked at me when I left, and she hadn't spoken a word to Brie either. If neither of us could get through to her, the man – or men – who'd hurt her would get away with it. There was always a possibility of physical evidence, especially since she'd allowed a rape kit, but if she refused to follow through on pressing charges, it wouldn't matter.

The thing was, I didn't think she was refusing to talk

because she wanted to be difficult. My gut said that she wasn't being sullen or rebellious or just being a teenager. She was scared. Not just of what had happened to her, but who had done it.

But until she was ready to talk, there was nothing else I could do.

"Visiting?" The Lyft driver asked as I settled in the backseat. "Nothing too serious, I hope."

It was on the tip of my tongue to snap back that I'd spent the night at the bedside of a fourteen-year-old girl who'd been brutally assaulted, but he didn't deserve it. He was simply trying to make small talk. He sucked at it, but he was making an effort.

I gave him a tired smile and my address, hoping my lack of an answer would be hint enough that I didn't want to talk. Fortunately, it was, and the only sound for the rest of the ride back to my place was the low murmur of classical music from the radio. I gave him an extra tip when we arrived and then plodded up the stairs, barely having the energy to lift my feet.

Mai was sitting at the table when I entered, but before the door even shut behind me, she was up and hugging me. I leaned into her, accepting the comfort and strength she offered. I didn't think I could stay on my feet without it.

"Do you want to talk about it?" Mai asked as she let me go.

I shook my head. "It was...bad."

"I'm scheduled to work, and then Hob and I were going to spend the whole night together, but I can call off and tell him we'll do it another time." She walked with me to the kitchen and set water on to boil before going into the cupboard to get a tea bag.

The fact that she knew I'd want tea made tears well up. I might not have had a family growing up, but I had one now. No matter how alone I felt, I wasn't going through this by myself. I needed to take my own advice and stop acting as if I had to carry the weight of the world all alone.

Still, what I needed right now wasn't Mai's companionship, but rather a shower and a nap. She didn't need to be home for that.

"I'm going to clean up, get something to eat, then sleep for twenty hours." I leaned against the counter. "So be prepared for tomorrow night to be a girls' night in."

She smiled. "I'll pick up some Rocky Road on my way home tomorrow."

"Thank you," I said, reaching out to squeeze her hand. "It means a lot to me that you're willing to change your plans."

"Of course." She poured the now-boiling water into

a mug and dropped the tea bag in. "It's what family does."

I was starting to see that.

She stayed long enough for me to drink my tea before leaving, making me promise to call if I needed her. When the door shut behind her, the apartment was completely quiet. It wouldn't be long before the neighboring apartments filled up with people coming back from work and kids coming home from school, but for right now, the silence was a relief.

Sort of.

Without anything to distract me and being too tired to fight, thoughts started popping up in my mind. Soleil was safe, and all I could do was wait to see what she decided to do. We had reached a point where I had done all I could. That meant another worry had room to creep up on me.

Evanne.

I hadn't really expected Alec to keep me in the loop, not with how we'd left things between us, but that didn't mean I no longer cared what was going on with Evanne. She meant a lot to me, no matter what was going on with Alec and me, and I wanted to know that she was safe.

Maybe if I'd been a little more awake, I would've overthought things or come up with valid reasons why this wasn't a good idea, but I had been functioning on too little sleep for too many days. I dug my phone out of my purse and typed out a message to Alec.

I was just wondering if Keli had brought Evanne back yet. I wasn't in school today to see if Evanne was back or not.

It might've been abrupt, but I wasn't going to get into anything else with him, especially over text when I was this tired. I just wanted to know that Evanne was okay. As for everything else, that was a problem for a different day. Today's problem was done, and I needed to sleep.

As tempting as it was to linger in the shower, I knew if I did that, I risked falling asleep and not waking up until I used up all the hot water in the building. That would definitely *not* make my day any better. Or anyone else's, for that matter. Still, the hot water helped relax me some.

I went for a simple meal, not having the energy to make much of anything else. After nothing but shit food for the past couple days, even my grilled cheese sandwich tasted gourmet. I barely finished it before my eyelids got too heavy to keep up. I curled up, pulling an afghan over me even as I fell asleep.

Sand and pebbles shifted under my thin-soled shoes as I walked, and the sound of the waves against the shore rolled over me. I liked it out here. The smell of the saltwater. The birds overhead. Kids laughing.

It was a treat, they'd said. A trip to the beach before school started as a reward for behaving so well over the summer. They'd been promising it since school let out, and I knew I wasn't the only one who saw the trip for what it was. A bribe. But it was one they at least followed through with, which made them more honest than a lot of other foster parents I'd had in the last four years.

We weren't the only ones out today. It was a rare day weather-wise, with the sun out and the temperature actually warm enough for us to go into the water. Some of the others were here alone or with groups of friends, but at least half a dozen were families.

Parents with little kids, older kids, teenagers. All different colors and sizes. Some of them were yelling and some were laughing and some were just talking. Even the ones who didn't look happy, I envied. Because they were together.

The parents wanted their kids. They chose to spend the time and money – little as it may have cost them – to have a day at the beach together rather than choosing something selfish.

Like my parents had.

I liked watching the parents with the kids. How they talked to each other. How they played together. A Frisbee between three of them. A football for Monkey in the

Middle. *Sandcastles and digging holes. Picking up shells and rocks worn smooth by the tides.*

I stooped to pick one up, carried it with me, but I knew it wouldn't be coming back with me. Small as it was, I didn't need to add something else to drag along with me the next time I moved.

People didn't understand that most of the time. They didn't understand that, for kids like me, going to a new foster home wasn't like when a family moved. We didn't get suitcases and boxes to pack up all our clothes and toys and books and other worldly possessions. We got a trash bag and a reminder that we didn't know how much space we'd have wherever we were going. Better to take as little as possible. Less to have to choose between and less to lose.

"Lumen!"

I turned at the sound of my name, wondering who was calling me. I knew the voice, but it didn't belong here. It wasn't this here and now. It was the other. But I knew it all the same.

"Lumen!"

Who was–

"What?" I sat up too fast, and my head spun.

Someone was knocking on my door and shouting my name. My brain was clear enough for me to know that I recognized the voice, but I wasn't quite awake enough yet to put a name to it.

By the time I stumbled over, I remembered, but it didn't stop me from opening the door.

"Alec."

TWELVE
ALEC

No warrant. No help. Nothing but more *I'm sorry, we can't* excuses. Nothing but reasons why this wasn't considered anything more serious than a custody issue when we all knew that if the situation had been reversed and I had been the one to take our daughter while Keli'd had custody, a warrant would have already been out for my arrest on charges of kidnapping.

I'd gone straight from the police station to meet Percival Scarpa, where he'd agreed with my scathing opinion regarding how the issue was being handled. He'd also agreed that maybe it was time to play to the press.

When I asked him, however, about how I should go about doing just that, he'd asked if I had a public relations person. He had been able to give me legal advice but recommended that I speak to a PR person regarding what, exactly, should be said.

After leaving his office, I'd reached out to the firm that handled all of the public relations for my family. Of course, they'd been able to see me, but our meeting had been brief. They hadn't needed much from me, and I'd asked them to reach out to Theresa for the person I wanted to be the face for the media.

I should have been grateful that had gone so well, but now all I had to look forward to was a night of worrying and pacing, with nothing to distract me. Eoin was still out checking various car rental places, but I didn't have anything else to do. The money trail I'd been sent to investigate didn't exist. Keli hadn't been using any of the credit cards that my money manager had access to, and without a warrant, nothing in her name could be tracked.

Fortunately for me, Brody was waiting in my living room when I arrived home.

And he'd brought alcohol.

"I have a new batch of whiskey I thought might be useful here." He poured two fingers of rich-looking amber liquid and handed me the glass. "Mind helping me test it?"

"Aye." I took the glass. "I hope you brought plenty."

BRODY HAD INDEED BROUGHT plenty of his newest whiskey, and it was excellent. I probably would have drunk just as much if it hadn't been of good quality, but I wouldn't have enjoyed it as much. I'd most likely regret it in the morning, but I was tired of constantly planning and looking ahead, especially since it no longer appeared that I could better control outcomes no matter what I did.

"A wee nip more." I held out my glass.

"You dinnae need more," Brody cautioned.

"*Pog mo thon.*" I scowled at him.

"Gaelic? Really, Alec?" Brody stood. "I'm going to the bathroom, and then I'll be making us both some coffee."

I flipped up my middle finger. "That American enough for you?"

He rolled his eyes and headed for the hall.

I suddenly realized that I hadn't checked my phone in hours, and I reached for it. My stomach churned unpleasantly when I saw that I'd missed a text from Lumen.

She wanted to know about Evanne.

I should have been pissed about that, but instead, all I could think about was how good it would feel to have her in my arms. How much better she was than even this fine whiskey. How I could lose myself in her more thoroughly than anything else.

I needed her.

Now.

I glanced in the direction Brody had gone. If I wanted to go to her, I needed to go now because Brody would try to stop me. He wouldn't understand.

I could do this. Grab a taxi. Go to Lumen's.

I'd answer her question in person.

Twenty minutes later, there I was.

"Alec?"

Lumen sounded surprised to see me, which I found endearing. I took a step toward her. "You texted me."

The puzzled expression on her face didn't change.

"Fuck it." I'd always been better with action than words.

I reached for her, my mouth coming down on hers even as my hands cupped her face. Damn it all to hell. She was too sweet. Too soft. I had been without her for too long–

She shoved me back, and I hit her doorframe. "What the *hell* was that?!"

"A kiss." I grinned at her. "I'll show you again."

I made to move forward again, but this time, she put her hand out, stopping me. I frowned.

"You're drunk."

"Pfft." I gave a dismissive wave. "I'm a Scot. Ya ken we cannae get drunk off a wee bit o' whiskey. 'Tis like water for us. I could swim in it an' still be sober as a priest on Sunday."

"Somehow, I doubt that. You smell like you swam in it."

I raised my arm and sniffed. "Aye, I suppose I had more'n a wee bit."

"And you decided to show up here, uninvited and drunk, because...?"

"Message!" I said triumphantly.

Her face lit up with hope. "Evanne's home?"

I scowled. "No."

"So, you came to answer my text in person?"

"I came to see you, lass," I said. "Need to get my mind off the whole bloody business and nothin' does that as well as a good fuck. An' you're a great fuck."

She crossed her arms. "You're an ass."

"But I have a sexy arse." I winked at her...and then promptly threw up on the rug.

THIRTEEN
LUMEN

"You've got to be kidding me."

When he'd kissed me, a thousand things had gone through my head at the same time, not the least of which was how good it felt, how right. But following quick on that thought had been the taste of alcohol, and it had been that more than anything else that had cleared my head.

It became clear rather quickly after that the real reason he'd come. Not to apologize or ask about Soleil. He hadn't even really come to tell me about Evanne. He'd come because he was drunk and horny, and that had somehow made him think I'd fall into his arms and then into bed.

"Shite. Sorry. I'm such a fuck up."

His voice broke on the last word, and my anger gave

way to sympathy. Our fight hadn't meant that I'd thought Evanne's situation wasn't stressful or problematic. I was worried about her too and hoped that Keli would come to her senses and see that what she was doing wasn't good for her daughter.

"Let's get you cleaned up," I said, putting my hand on his shoulder. "Please tell me you didn't drive here."

He straightened, his face turned away in what I assumed was embarrassment. "I'm not that much of a fuck up. I took a cab."

"You're not a fuck up," I said as I led him over to the kitchen sink. I pulled a glass out of the cupboard and filled it with water before handing it to him. "Rinse your mouth out. Drink some water. I'm going to clean up the mess."

"I'm sorry, lass." He took a small sip. "I shouldn't even be here."

"It's understandable," I said as I gathered cleaning supplies from the hall closet. "This hasn't exactly been a great past couple days for you."

"I cannae figure out how I didn't see this coming. Keli and I hadn't dated a long time, but we have a child together. I should have seen that something was wrong."

"Do you think she planned it?" I asked as I sprayed cleaner onto the rug. Fortunately, Mai and I had bought this particular rug to keep in front of the door to keep us from tracking in mud and water, so it was made for easy cleaning.

"Doesna seem like it. But now she's on the move. Canceled her phone number."

That was alarming. "Have you gone to the police?"

"Aye. Right lot of good that did me. Why I drank so much."

"Have you had anything to eat today?" Based on the mess I was cleaning up, I felt confident that I knew the answer to my question, but I asked it anyway.

"I dinnae ken. Not hungry."

"Have you slept at all?"

"A bit here and there. I cannae get my brain to turn off."

"Is that another reason why you were drinking?"

"Aye." His eyes swept over my body. "And why I came here."

I bristled. "Right, because you wanted someone to fuck." I carried my things back into the kitchen.

"Because I missed you, lass." He didn't look at me as he said it, but I could hear the sincerity in every word. "You're the only person I could think of who could take my mind off things."

It was a slightly sweeter sentiment than what he'd declared before, but this wasn't the time or place to follow that particular path of conversation. "Finish your water."

After he was done, I took him to the bathroom. His eyelids were already beginning to droop as I helped him take off his shirt and pants, and I wondered how much of this he'd remember in the morning. I cleaned him up as best I could short of a shower – if he fell asleep or passed out in there, I'd never get him out on my own – and gave him an extra toothbrush. He managed to brush his own teeth, and then I led him to my bedroom.

"I'll be right across the hall," I said as I sat him down on the bed. "Mai's staying with her boyfriend tonight, so I'm going to take her room."

He gave no sign that he'd heard me, but after he was under the covers, he reached out and grabbed my wrist. "Please, stay. I dinnae want to be alone."

I was tempted to be firm and tell him that wasn't happening, but the vulnerability in those beautiful blue eyes of his was too much to dismiss. "All right. I'll stay."

At least until he fell asleep. Once that happened, I'd make my escape. Waking up in bed next to him would send all sorts of wrong signals. Without bothering to change out of my leggings and t-shirt, I climbed into bed next to him and let him wrap his arm around me.

"If you throw up on me, you'll regret it." I used my best teacher voice.

"Won't. I promise." He pulled me closer, and I felt him relax against me.

This was going to be a very long night.

"EVANNE!"

I jerked awake at the shout, confusion fleeing the moment I remembered who was in my bed and why.

"Evanne!"

His body twisted as he yelled, limbs coming free as he threw the covers off. He thrashed, muttering other things that I couldn't quite make out. What was clear, however, was that he was caught in a nightmare.

"Alec." I grabbed his arm as it came toward me. When he yanked it back, I held on, nearly falling on top of him. My hands landed on his shoulders, and I shook him. "Alec! Wake up!"

"No!" Alec bolted upright so fast that our heads almost collided. His eyes were wide open, but for a few seconds, he didn't seem to see me or anything else.

"Alec, wake up." I shook him again.

He blinked and then frowned. "Lumen? What—?"

"It's okay. You were having a nightmare."

A shudder ran through his entire body, and pain

twisted his features. "Evanne. She accused me of abandoning her. Said she hated me."

"Shh." I put my hand on his cheek. The hurt on his face was breaking my heart. "It wasn't real."

"But it could be." He closed his eyes, leaning into my hand. "What if she comes back and hates me because I couldn't find her? What if she thinks I dinnae *want* to find her?"

I leaned forward and brushed my lips over his. Not a kiss driven by physical desire, but one meant to stop him from continuing along that self-destructive track.

"She knows you love her," I said firmly. "Evanne knows that you would do anything for her. She's a smart kid, and she loves her father very much."

His eyes opened, and they locked with mine. Clear and completely open for the first time, I could see into the depths of him, see the vulnerable parts that he tried to hide. I'd seen pieces of him before, this man who wanted nothing more than to take care of his family, but this was the first time I was seeing all of him. Maybe it was the alcohol or maybe the nightmare – more likely a combination of both – but his guard was down.

"I feel like the world is crashing down around me." He wrapped his hand around the back of my neck. "As if I have nothing to tether me here."

His thumb moved back and forth behind my ear,

heat spreading out from his touch. I didn't think he was even aware of doing it. It seemed more like he needed to touch me, as if the feel of skin on skin soothed him. As if *I* soothed him. As if he needed *me* in a way that no one had ever needed me before.

He leaned toward me, and I knew I had the chance to stop him if I truly wanted to, and that should have been what I wanted. Except all I could think about was how sad he looked right now and how much I wanted to take that expression off his face.

As his lips met mine, I had to admit that he wasn't the only one who needed this. After everything that'd happened these last few days, I craved his touch too.

I reached for him, making the sort of noise that would've been embarrassing if I'd taken the time to think about it. My palms slid up his chest, bare skin hot under my hands. His tongue slid into my mouth, thoroughly exploring as his hands dropped to my waist. He pulled me onto his lap, fingers fisting the fabric of my t-shirt. I raked my nails down his chest, earning a growl as they scraped his nipples. His fingers tightened, digging into my waist before moving down to tug at my leggings.

I leaned back, breaking the kiss.

"*Mhurninn,*" he protested, desperation in the word.

"Pants." I didn't bother trying to be sexy about it, my gut saying that it wouldn't take much for the mood to be lost, and the last thing I wanted was for this to be as insanely awkward as was inevitable. If I was going to be uncomfortable later, at least I could get an orgasm out of it.

Once I had my leggings off, I went back to his arms, letting him pull me back onto his lap. His mouth crashed into mine, hands palming my ass over my panties. He nipped at my bottom lip, and I rocked against him, moaning at the feel of him hardening under me.

His mouth moved across my jaw and down my throat. I shifted to give him better access, little tingles of electricity following the path of his lips. The majority of my attention, however, was focused somewhere else. I reached down between us, cupping him through his boxer briefs. His cock swelled even more, and I gave him a squeeze.

"Fuck," he groaned, fingers kneading my back. "Need you."

I couldn't agree more.

It took me only a few seconds to pull him out and move aside my underwear. Then I was rising up, positioning myself over his cock. I gasped as I sank down, the stretch almost painful as my body struggled to adjust. His hands slid over my ass and down my thighs, wrapping my legs around him.

"Shit, Alec." I closed my eyes, the new angle putting

pressure and friction in all the right places. My muscles trembled with the intensity of the sensations coursing through me.

"*Mo nighean bhan.*"

The now-familiar words sent a shiver down my spine, and I rocked against him, chasing the feeling. I didn't want to feel tenderness. I just needed to fill the ache growing inside me.

Alec, at least, seemed to be on the same page. One hand slid down my spine to the small of my back, urging me faster and faster. My forehead rested against his, ragged breathing mingling.

We were both wound so tight that I was already on the edge, and every inch of Alec's body was coiled and tense. I ground down on him, eliciting a groan and a curse.

"So close..." I breathed.

"Aye, lass. Come for me. Come on my cock, lass."

Pleasure exploded through me, and my back arched, head falling back. I cried out his name, pussy clamping down on him tight enough for another curse, and then he was coming too. We rode the wave together, letting the ecstasy chase away everything else until we existed only in a cloud of bliss.

FOURTEEN
LUMEN

WELL, THAT HAD BEEN A BIG FUCKING MISTAKE. Literally as well as figuratively. I should have known better.

I *had* known better.

I just hadn't wanted to listen. I'd wanted him.

We'd fallen asleep after, and I'd woken up first, just after dawn. He'd still been sleeping, and considering the alcohol he'd had on top of the stress of the past couple days and our late-night workout, I figured he'd be out for a while yet. That, at least, had given me time to shower, dress, and get some coffee going before I let my decisions from last night catch up with me.

I should have just sent him home. He hadn't driven, and he'd been coherent enough to take a cab home again. If I'd really been worried, I could've gone back with him, gotten him into his own bed, and then come back home. He would've had no problem paying for the trip.

But I hadn't done the smart thing. I'd let him stay, had taken care of him. And then I'd let his vulnerability get to me. He hadn't manipulated me. I refused to put all the responsibility on him. This was on me more than him. I'd been an idiot, and now I had to deal with the fallout.

Fallout that was sure to come soon now that Alec was in the bathroom taking a shower.

I busied myself with making toast even though I wasn't actually hungry. I needed something in my stomach other than coffee, and Alec probably did too. I doubted either of us would be able to stomach something that wasn't bland despite the fact that I hadn't been drunk. I didn't want a repeat of yesterday's mess.

Speaking of mess...

Heat flooded my face as I remembered why I'd need to wash my sheets today. We'd been so caught up in the moment that we hadn't used a condom. I didn't even have alcohol as an excuse. Fortunately, I trusted that Alec was clean, and I was covered on the pregnancy front. Still, it shouldn't have even been an issue to begin with. It had been careless of me.

"I don't suppose Mai's boyfriend has a shirt lying around here I can use, does he?" Alec asked as he came into the kitchen. He wore the same pants as last night, but no shirt, and the sight of his bare chest made all sorts of things inside me squirm.

"I'll check." As I passed him, I added, "help yourself to the toast and coffee."

Hob usually kept a few extra things in Mai's closet for the rare occasions he ended up staying without having brought clothes with him. He was shorter than Alec by several inches, but it was still better than offering one of my shirts. I found a plain t-shirt and made a mental note to buy Hob a new one. When I returned to the kitchen, Alec was sitting at the table, grimacing as he chewed.

"Need something for your head?" I asked as I held out the shirt. As much as I enjoyed seeing him without a shirt, I needed him to cover up so I could remember why last night had been a bad idea all the way around. My libido didn't always work well with sensibility.

"No, thank you. I took some ibuprofen from a bottle in the bathroom cabinet." He drained the last of a glass of water and then took a drink of coffee. "I owe you an apology."

"All right." I moved over to the table and took the seat across from him.

"I shouldn't have come here last night." He looked at me, and I saw that his shields were back in place. "My brother, Brody, makes scotch, and he thought trying a new batch would be the best way to distract me from the lack of progress in finding Evanne."

"That's understandable." I wrapped my hands around my mug. "You've been under a lot of stress recently."

"Still, receiving your message should not have led me to thinking it was appropriate to show up here." He glanced toward the door. "I'll replace the rug."

"It's fine." I met his gaze. "The rug isn't really the main issue here."

"Aye, you're right." He finished the last of his coffee and took his mug to the sink. I waited for him to say something else, but he didn't.

"I appreciate the apology for showing up here drunk, but we still need to talk about the things you said before."

He turned, expression a careful mask. "I have no more to say on the subject."

"Are you serious?" I was on my feet in an instant. "How can you act like what you said wasn't hurtful?"

"I don't see the point in bringing it up again," he said. "Not when you won't admit how wrong your actions were."

"Excuse me?" I stared at him. His changing moods

gave me whiplash, and I wasn't in the best state of mind to deal with that right now.

"You wanted me to prioritize a stranger over my own daughter, and I see now how you can't understand what was wrong with that. You don't have a family."

I took a step back, his words a slap in my face. My hands curled into fists. "You privileged bastard! Trust me, I can relate to your situation a hell of a lot better than you could understand mine. If you had even a clue of what it's like to be a kid in the system, you would have understood why I wanted to look for Soleil instead of Evanne."

"Evanne is my daughter. You cannae stand there and tell me that I should have put a stranger's well-being over that of my own child—"

I held up a hand, barely holding back my temper. "I *never* said you needed to put Soleil over Evanne, only that *I* was going to look for Soleil. You had no right to criticize my decision."

"You're the one who kept havering on about this missing girl while I was trying to figure out how to get my daughter back."

I pointed my finger at him. "No. You don't get to do that. You don't get to twist around what I said to make it sound like I'd wanted you to focus all of your time and energy on finding Soleil. I was worried about Evanne too. I didn't think a small bit of concern was unreasonable." I shook my head. "It shouldn't have been too much to ask, but you decided where *both* of our priorities should be, and you didn't like that I didn't agree."

"Because you're wrong," he snapped. "There's a difference between a child being taken against her will and a teenager getting herself into trouble because she hung out with the wrong crowd or put herself in the wrong place at the wrong time."

"You're right. There's a difference in the two situations." Anger simmered just below the surface, and I knew I wouldn't be able to hold it back much longer. "A child being taken by a mother who loves her and will protect her versus a scared, angry teenager who has problems a self-absorbed asshole like you couldn't begin to fathom."

"Just because I wasn't in the foster system doesna mean I had a trouble-free childhood," he countered.

I threw up my hands. "I don't know why I'm even bothering. Men like you see the world your way, and anything that doesn't fit into that world view is cast aside like it's not even worth your attention."

"Don't you dare pretend you ken a single thing about me." His voice was as dark as his expression.

"But I do," I said, my voice a low growl. "That's what

you don't get. I've known people like you my entire life. I'd just thought you were different. Now, I know better."

A knock on my door stopped any response from him and gave me a few seconds to clamp down on the emotions threatening to spill over. I needed to get him out of here sooner rather than later, or things would get worse than they already were.

FIFTEEN

ALEC

I followed Lumen to the door. Who was knocking on her door on a Saturday morning? A spike of something too close to jealousy went through me. I had a vague memory of her saying that her roommate had stayed elsewhere last night, which meant it likely was someone for Lumen.

When the door opened, however, I realized that the people on the other side were actually here for me.

"What are you doing here?" I asked.

Lumen turned and looked at me. "Your brothers?"

"Aye. Eoin and Brody."

"I remember that one." She pointed at Eoin as she turned back to them. "Good timing. Get your brother out of my place."

"I should beat your ass for leaving without telling

me," Brody said, looking over Lumen's head at me. "What the hell were you thinking?"

"He wasn't," Eoin answered for me. "At least not with his big head."

His gaze slid to Lumen, and I gritted my teeth. I didn't want him looking at her or vice versa. He'd always been the kind of guy who'd had his fair share of attention from women, and the scar he'd received overseas only added to his hero appeal. If any man could live up to her ideal, it would be him, and despite the argument we'd been having only moments before, I didn't like the idea of her and my brother being attracted to each other.

"May we come in?" Brody directed the question to Lumen, giving her that charming smile that had entranced so many women.

Bastard.

"As long as it's to get his ass out of here," Lumen said, jerking her thumb at me.

Eoin and Brody stepped past Lumen without a response to her statement, and I moved over to where my shoes sat a few feet away from the door. She could throw away my shirt, but I wanted my shoes.

"I found someone who was willing to do me a favor," Eoin said. "He pulled some strings and got information from the rental place."

Everything else became unimportant as I focused on what my brother was saying. "You found them?"

"I think so," he said. "The car hasn't been returned yet, and GPS shows it in Portland, Oregon."

Portland.

"Evanne's in Portland?" Lumen asked.

The expression on her face struck me. No matter that I'd just accused her of not caring about Evanne, I'd known in my gut that wasn't the truth. She might've placed another person's well-being ahead of my daughter's, but that didn't mean Lumen didn't care about Evanne at all.

"The car is still registered to Keli, and her card is the one on file to charge, so unless the rental place failed to check the car in, settle Keli's bill, and then check the car out again, then she's still the one using it." Eoin answered Lumen's question, but he spoke to me while he did it.

"Do you have an address?" I asked, not wanting to get my hopes up too high. Narrowing it down to Portland was great, but it still didn't mean we could show up right where Keli was. I had no idea how accurate a rental car's GPS could be.

"We do," he said. "The tracking system is accurate within a few feet, and it looks like the car's been parked at a hotel for the past few hours."

That made sense. Keli wasn't the sort of woman who would have slept in her car to avoid detection. She'd want access to a bed and a shower. And that wasn't even taking Evanne into consideration. While my daughter occasionally enjoyed playing at camping or skipping a bath every so often, I doubted she would take being confined to a car without the comforts of home very well.

"What's our next step?" I asked.

"Knowing where they are won't change what the police are able to do," Brody said.

Eoin shoved his hands in his pockets. "Even if we asked the cops here if they would be willing to go with us or reach out to Portland PD, Keli could turn the tables on you, make it seem like you've been stalking her. With people around to play to, she could act as if she's scared of you, and the police might believe her."

I didn't need more frustration. I needed answers. "What do we do then?"

"Eoin thinks we should go to the hotel, the three of us, and once Evanne sees you, she'll come to you. With the two of us there, Keli shouldn't do anything stupid. Once you have Evanne, it's just a matter of taking her to the car and bringing her home."

Brody made it sound so easy.

"We don't know how long they'll be there," Eoin said. "We need to get on the road."

It wasn't until Lumen cleared her throat behind me that I remembered where we were and who was with us.

And the argument we'd been having only a few minutes ago.

Shite.

I didn't want to leave things like this between us. Her last words about how she'd thought I was different, but now that she knew better, they stung. More than stung, if I was being honest with myself. I didn't like that she thought those things of me. I needed her to see how wrong she was about me, about this situation.

"Come with us."

Her eyebrows shot up. "What?"

"What are you doing?" Eoin looked at me like I was crazy. "This isn't a road trip."

I ignored him. "Come with me to get Evanne. I know she'll be glad to see you. And we can...talk."

Her gaze moved from one brother to the other before coming back to me. She crossed her arms. "I don't think we need an audience, and I don't have anything else to say."

I didn't believe that, but saying so would only put her even more on the defensive. "I have a few things to add."

Her expression cooled, and her eyes narrowed. "Well, this isn't all about you, is it?"

My brothers moved behind me, and I didn't have to look at them to know how uncomfortable they were at the conversation.

"Besides, I have to stay here in case Soleil needs me."

The same girl who'd gone missing before. I hadn't asked Lumen about whether or not the girl had been found, and if she had, what the circumstances had been. Was that proof of what Lumen had been saying, that the reason Lumen had to look for Soleil was because no one else cared that a foster girl was missing?

"Well, now that you're not waiting on me, you can leave." Lumen jerked her chin toward the door. Then she hesitated, expression softening. "I hope Evanne's there, and you get her back."

"But you don't want to come with us."

She shook her head. "Like I said, I need to be here for Soleil."

Of course.

If that's where her priorities were, I wouldn't keep her from it. Without bothering to say anything else, I turned and walked away. My brothers followed, and the sound of the door closing behind them echoed in my head. I pushed it away, though. I was too close to getting Evanne back to let anything distract me again.

SIXTEEN
LUMEN

WHAT. THE. HELL.

Was I ever going to have a nice, boring weekend? Or a boring week, for that matter? Honestly, the way this school year had been going, I was beginning to wonder if this was just what my life was going to be, moving from one moment of confusion and chaos to another, in both my professional and personal lives.

Getting involved with Alec McCrae had been a huge mistake. I should have known the moment he'd walked into Real Life Bodywork that he'd derail the plans I had in place for my life. There had been so many red flags. I really had no one to blame but myself.

The realization only made me feel worse, especially since I knew I still cared about Alec. I still wanted him.

I pulled my hair back into a ponytail and went back

to the kitchen to clean up. I had some grading to do, and lesson plans to write, but I wasn't in any frame of mind to do that. What I could do, however, was find physical things to do. Like cleaning and doing laundry. Both were things that needed to be done, and all the anger I'd had bubbling up inside me needed to get out somehow. Being constructive seemed like the best way to handle things.

Once I was done with the kitchen, I moved into my bedroom. Still standing in the doorway, I took a deep breath, trying to steady myself, but as the scent of him filled my lungs, all it did was bring back images from last night, vivid enough to make my body tingle.

The soft cotton of my t-shirt rubbing against my hard nipples.

The sting of his teeth on my throat.

The stubble on his jaw chafing my skin.

His thick shaft pulsing inside me.

Fuck.

I forced my feet to carry me over to my bed, and I stripped it completely, tossing the sheets and blankets to the floor. I wasn't sure which would be better, to keep my breathing shallow to take in less of his scent or to keep breathing deep in order to desensitize myself to it.

I should have slept in Mai's room like I'd planned. I still would've wanted to wash my sheets, but at least I wouldn't have needed to deal with the scent of sex along with everything else. Even the tinge of alcohol from his sweat couldn't cover it up.

With the washers and dryers in the basement, I didn't have the luxury of staying in my apartment if I wanted to sleep on clean sheets tonight. Besides, running up and down the stairs sounded like a good way to burn off some of the adrenaline still in my system.

While waiting for the washer to do its thing, I went back up to the apartment to start cleaning the living room. The problem with the sort of cleaning I could do blindfolded was that it didn't take much brain power, and that meant my brain needed to find other things to do. Unfortunately, it wanted to focus on the last thing I wanted to think about.

Alec.

The first time I'd seen him, coming in out of the rain, I'd been struck by how good-looking he was. For the first time ever, I'd been tempted by a client.

That should have been my first clue to get the hell away from him.

Instead, I'd played nice and learned how gorgeous the body beneath the expensive suit was. The fancy, intricate cross that covered his back. The initials SAM that I had later learned belonged to his mother.

I'd loved touching him. I couldn't deny it.

But I still should have known better.

Then he'd asked about a 'happy ending,' and I'd felt justified in sending him away. That should have been the end.

Except he'd come back.

Why had I let him back in? I could've been fine with accepting an apology. Why had I gone further? Why had I taken him home with me? Why had I kept seeing him after I found out he was the father of one of my students?

I was an idiot.

That pretty much had to be it because I couldn't see another explanation that made sense. I had no one to blame but myself. I'd known that he and I came from vastly different worlds and that he hadn't been looking for a relationship. Despite all the proof I'd seen over the years about how stories like this really ended, I'd been foolish enough to believe we could be different.

It didn't matter how right we'd felt together or how well we'd seemed to get along. The truth was, the world didn't work that way. People like me had to work their asses off to get a good life, and people like him had it handed to them.

None of this stopped my heart from skipping when the front door opened. No logic regarding the fact that he didn't have a key could stop my mind from immediately leaping to the conclusion that Alec had come back. No rational thinking kept me from being disappointed when it was Mai instead.

She stopped at the spot where our rug used to be, looked down, looked up at me, then around the apartment. "Did I miss something?"

I sighed and sat on the floor, abandoning the rag I'd been using to clean and polish the end table next to the couch. "You have no idea."

Mai took off her shoes, dropped her purse and overnight bag on the floor, and came over to sit next to me. "Start with where our rug is and why it's gone. I have a feeling it's related to your sudden need to polish a table we picked up at a flea market for five bucks."

"Alec showed up last night, drunk."

Mai's eyes widened, but she didn't say anything.

"He said he missed me, kissed me, and then threw up all over the rug. It's in the bathroom now."

The horrified expression on her face made me feel better. At least I wasn't alone in thinking the past eighteen hours or so had been completely insane.

"Is he still here?" She whispered the question, eyes darting toward the hallway.

I shook my head.

"You sent him home after he threw up?"

I shook my head again.

Her expression softened, worry competing with compassion. "Oh, sweetie. Did you sleep with him?"

"I didn't mean to." I scrubbed my face with my hands. "After he threw up, I got him and the rug cleaned up, but I didn't want to send him home like that. He'd taken a cab here, and I could've sent him back in one, but I didn't know if he'd pass out or not."

"Not sure how cleaning up puke turned into you accidentally fucking him."

Leave it to Mai to boil a situation down to the most basic elements.

"I put him in my bed and figured I'd sleep in yours."

She wrinkled her nose. "Now, I'm hoping you kept the action to your room."

I gave her a withering look. "I wouldn't have sex in your bed."

She shrugged. "The whole thing is weird. I didn't want to make assumptions."

She had a point.

"He asked me to stay with him, so I figured I'd stay until he fell asleep. With how insane my last couple days have been, I was exhausted. I fell asleep too and then woke up with him yelling Evanne's name." Despite everything, my heart twisted with the memory. "I woke him up, and he told me he'd had a nightmare."

"Ah." Mai got it. "The whole nightmare-turns-to-comfort-sex sort of 'accident.'"

I blinked. "What was that?"

She grinned at me. "Come on, don't you pick up anything from rom-coms? The hero has a nightmare, and the heroine tries to comfort him, which turns into sex."

I frowned. "Why is he the hero?"

"Okay, you can be the hero comforting the heroine."

I rolled my eyes. "I'm glad this amuses you."

"What is it you always say? Find the humor and the light where you can."

"I didn't think that would apply to my sex life," I said. "But it does make me feel a bit better."

Mai wrapped her arm around my shoulder and hugged me. "Everyone makes sex mistakes. It's part of growing up."

"I must've missed that day in adulting school." I leaned against her, grateful for her support.

"I'll lend you my notes."

"When did you make a sex mistake?" I asked, suddenly curious.

"When I was a senior in high school, I slept with one of Ru's friends." She shook her head and laughed. "Trust me on this, never date your siblings' friends or your friends' siblings. It doesn't end well."

"I'm surprised Ru didn't beat the shit out of the guy."

"He wanted to," she admitted. "But then I told him I'd seduced the poor bastard...and then broke things off with him two days later. Ru figured that was punishment enough."

We sat together for a while before Mai finally released me. She kissed my forehead. "What do you need me to do?"

"This was it," I said. "Right now, I'm going to keep cleaning because I want to tire myself out. If I don't, chances are I won't sleep tonight."

Mai held out a hand and helped me to my feet. "You don't expect me to clean too, do you?"

I laughed. "No. You do whatever you planned to do today."

"I figured I'd get a head start on the week and prep some easy meals before we have our girls' night."

"Perfect. You make a mess, and I'll clean it up." Even as I said it, I realized that's what I did too often. Cleaned up other people's messes. I needed to be careful that I didn't fall into that pattern with Soleil. There was a fine line between helping and enabling. I didn't want to blur it.

With Mai there, it was easier to keep from thinking too much. She talked about everything, letting me answer when I felt like it or be quiet when I wanted to. The time flew by, and before I knew it, I was in the shower, cleaning off all the grime and sweat of the day and preparing to crash for the night. Food and binge-watching a comedy with Mai seemed like the best way to do it.

Life, however, seemed to have other plans.

As I was helping Mai clear the table after dinner, my phone rang. My heart thudded against my ribcage as I reached for the phone, but the screen showed the last name I'd expected.

Josalyn.

Shit.

Something had happened to Soleil.

SEVENTEEN
ALEC

Neither of my brothers trusted me to drive, and I couldn't really blame them, not after the completely immature way I'd handled things last night and this morning. I still didn't want to believe I'd been such an idiot. I could count on one hand the number of times I had actually been drunk in my life, and the other times had ended with me hugging a toilet, not showing up at a woman's house and making a fool of myself.

Despite the three-and-a-half-hour drive, I didn't have much time to think about any of this since Eoin was sleeping in the back, and Brody was driving. When Brody drove, he liked to either talk...or sing. My brother had a lot of talents, but music wasn't one of them. Not only was he completely tone deaf, but he had no rhythm, not when it came to music anyway. And he never knew the lyrics.

None of that, however, stopped him from torturing people whenever the need struck him. Such as when he was in the car, and his passengers didn't want to talk.

"...could we dial forty cents, we were merely freshmen..." He grinned at me.

"I'm fairly certain that is not the lyric." I sighed. "But you're going to continue singing them wrong until I agree to talk about what happened last night between Lumen and myself, aren't you?"

"Well, I do have an entire song list just waiting to be massacred."

I hated that grin. It meant he was up to something. In this case, at least, I knew what he was up to. He wanted me to talk, and he knew how to make that happen.

"You're a right bastard, you know that." I shifted positions in the seat. "What do you want to know?"

"She looked pretty pissed at you earlier, but you'd been there all night."

"That's not a question."

"Don't be a smartass."

"I went there last night, pissed enough to think it was a grand idea. I kissed her and then threw up on her rug."

"And she slept with you?" He shook his head. "Damn. How do you not have more women falling all over you?"

"It wasn't like that." I explained what happened without going into graphic detail. What Lumen and I had done together was personal, intimate. It wasn't the sort of thing that I wanted to share, no matter how confusing my feelings about her were at the moment.

When I was done, he gave me a concerned look. "Does that mean it's over between the two of you?"

"I don't know," I said honestly. "I can't be with someone who isn't willing to make Evanne a priority."

When Brody didn't respond after a minute or so, I looked over at him. He seemed focused on the road, but he wasn't singing or talking, which told me that something was on his mind. Most people thought Brody was a goof-off, the type of person who didn't have much going on in his head, but I knew him better than that. He saw far more than anyone realized.

"Tell me what you're thinking," I said finally. "Be honest."

He took another minute before replying, "I think you fucked up."

Well, that *was* honest.

"I'm not saying that Evanne shouldn't be your first priority, but you tend to think that everyone else has to revolve around the things in your life too." He shot me a glance. "It's not as if Lumen blew you off for something silly or pointless."

I glared at him. "If I'd known you would take her side, I would have told you to keep singing."

"Sometimes you need to hear the truth, even if you don't like it, big brother."

Fortunately for me, it was only a few minutes later when we pulled into a gas station, and Eoin woke up. With only forty-five minutes or so left to go, Brody dropped the subject and struck up a conversation with Eoin. What he'd said, however, stuck with me until we reached the hotel. Only then was I able to shift my focus to what I was going to do now.

As Brody parked the car, Eoin and I scanned the parking lot and the exterior of the hotel. It was nice, but not a five-star place, meaning it'd probably have some security, but not something so tight we had no hope of getting information. I didn't see any police cars around, and the lot only had a dozen cars or so.

"That's the rental car," Eoin said as we walked up to the doors. He cut behind Brody and me to walk next to the car. Without slowing, he slid his hand across the hood and then joined us again, not missing a single step. "Hood's cold."

The lobby was empty, and only one person stood

behind the front desk. The tall, dark-haired young man stared at his phone until we were right across from him. Only then did he put it down with a weary sigh.

"Welcome to the—"

"We're not here to rent a room," Eoin said.

The guy's gaze shifted from me to Eoin, and his eyes widened when he saw the scar. "Um...we don't keep cash on hand."

Brody rolled his eyes. "Relax, kid. We're not here to rob you or cause you any trouble." He leaned on the counter, fixing on his most charming smile. "Here's the thing. My brother here has this ex giving him problems. I'm sure you know what it's like. You break up with a girl, and she decides she wants to get back at you."

The guy's head bobbed up and down, as if he knew exactly what Brody was saying even though the way the tips of his ears reddened made me doubt he'd been involved with anyone long enough to have an 'ex.'

"This ex," Brody continued, "took my niece even though Alec has custody. I have papers to prove it."

Eoin handed over some papers I hadn't realized he was carrying. Brody put them on the counter and slid them across to the clerk. The kid's eyes dropped to them, then came back up to focus on Brody again.

"Now, we don't want her to get into trouble. That's why we came instead of calling the cops. We don't want this to be some big thing where it disturbs guests, probably brings down your supervisor and their supervisor." Brody straightened. "All we want is the room number. We'll go knock on the door. Say our piece. Nice and quiet."

I couldn't believe Brody could say that with a straight face. He never did anything 'nice and quiet.'

"You just want to talk?"

"Aye, lad. I just want to talk." My smile wasn't as charming as Brody's, but at least I wouldn't scare the kid as much as Eoin clearly did.

"Her name?"

I honestly couldn't believe this was working. "Keli Miller."

The kid typed on his keyboard for a minute and then whispered, "Three forty-six."

"Thanks." Brody slid a bill across the counter. "We appreciate it."

As we got onto the elevator, I asked, "Why did you pay him after he gave us what we wanted?"

"It'll keep him from calling the room and warning Keli because he had a sudden attack of conscience and realized it probably wasn't a good idea to give three strange men the room number where a single woman and child were staying."

"Good thinking," Eoin said.

"I don't like how easy that was," I said as the elevator doors opened on the third floor. "If someone wanted to get to me through Evanne, they could have done the exact same thing."

This was exactly why I had the best security tech money could buy. To keep Evanne safe. It was also one of the reasons I had never disputed the amount of money I gave to Keli. I had assumed she would use it the same way, putting our daughter's safety above all. The fact that Keli wouldn't use the money I knew she had to put her and Evanne at a place with better security added to my irritation.

When we reached the right room, both of my brothers looked to me. They'd done their part. Now it was time for me to take point.

I knocked on the door and waited, hoping Keli wouldn't force me to make a scene by not answering because I didn't intend to leave until I'd at least seen Evanne. I heard the deadbolt click, and then the door opened, security chain still in place.

"Really, Keli? Do you think I'm planning to force my way into the room?" I kept my voice even and calm.

"I don't know–"

"Daddy?" The familiar voice cut straight through me. "Daddy's here!"

"Just a minute, sweetie," Keli said with a sigh. "I have to unlock the door all the way."

A few seconds later, she moved aside, letting all three of us inside the room. I caught her glaring at my brothers, but then Evanne was throwing herself at me, and I bent to catch her. The moment she was in my arms, I forgot all about everything else and focused on her.

"I'm so glad to see you! Mommy said she didn't know when you were coming, and I told her it would be soon because I have school on Monday, and I didn't want more fun days."

"Fun days?"

"You know, instead of sick days. You call in *fun* instead of *sick*."

And now I understood how she'd kept Evanne from being upset about missing school. Pretending they were on some sort of vacation had allowed Keli to hide the truth of what was happening. At least I didn't need to worry about what to tell Evanne about what was going on. As long as Keli was willing to keep up the charade and let me take Evanne home without an argument, I wouldn't call Keli out on the lies.

Which meant I needed to talk to her in private.

"*Mo chride*, guess who came with me?" I turned us around so she could see Eoin and Brody.

"Uncle Brody! Uncle Eoin!"

She squirmed to get down, and I let her go. As she ran to them, I gestured for Keli to step into the bathroom with me. It wasn't ideal, but it was the best option available. Evanne was giggling like mad as I closed the door, and the sound made me smile. That smile disappeared, however, as I turned to face Keli.

"What the hell were you thinking?" I kept my voice low, not wanting Evanne to hear me.

To my shock – and dismay – Keli burst into tears.

Fuck.

As angry as I was, I hadn't meant to make her cry. It wasn't as if she'd done anything to hurt our daughter. A few days of vacation together, and now, Evanne would be going home. Still, I couldn't completely brush it aside, not unless I wanted to spend the next decade constantly wondering if she would do it again.

"Talk to me. Tell me what made you do this."

"Alessandro dumped me."

I frowned. "I don't follow."

She sat down on the edge of the bathtub and pulled a few tissues from the box on the sink counter. "By the third day in Italy, I missed Evanne. By the end of the week, I'd decided to try to convince Alex that she should come live with us."

Since that was no longer an issue, I decided against telling her that I never would have let that happen.

"Two days before I came back, he and I had a huge fight. He said that he hadn't signed up for a kid and that no man wants another guy's brat around. Then he said that if I hadn't been such a good lay, he never would've asked me out in the first place."

He had been a bigger asshole than I originally thought.

"The entire flight back, all I could think of was that if no man would want another guy's child, then to get the family I wanted, it had to be you, Evanne, and me. We could make things work." She wiped at her cheeks and then blew her nose. Her eyes were red, but she'd stopped crying. "Then when you said you didn't want to be with me, I got scared that I was going to lose Evanne to you and your new girlfriend, all because I made one stupid choice. The three of you would be your own family, and I'd be forgotten."

I didn't want to be sympathetic after what she'd put me through, but I could see how she could have felt that she was losing Evanne.

"You're Evanne's mother. No one will ever take that away from you."

Keli's bottom lip trembled as she looked up at me. "I

saw how much she loves her teacher, and I panicked. I didn't have a plan. I just...freaked out."

In business, being able to read people separated the good from the great, and I was in the latter group. Having been surprised by Keli's actions actually made me more convinced that she was telling the truth. She'd acted on impulse, and things had snowballed from there. If I had to guess, she'd probably come straight here from the rental place and hadn't been able to figure out how to fix what she'd done.

"Are the police in the hall or the lobby?" Her voice was small as she dropped her head, shoulders slumping. "Please don't let Evanne see them arrest me. Not for me, but for her."

"No police," I said, glad for the first time that they hadn't been involved. "Not unless you intend on trying to take Evanne and run again."

She shook her head. "I'm so sorry, Alec. How do I make this right?"

My original intention to simply leave Keli here alone didn't take into account Keli's reasoning, or the fact that not having her around would make the legal aspect of this more complicated rather than less. It was time for a different plan.

"Well, to start, both of you are coming back to Seattle with us. You're going to stay in a hotel and

Evanne will come back home with me. Sunday is Halloween, and I promised her I would take her trick-or-treating. If you want to come with us, you can, but you're not going to be alone with her until I know for certain I can trust you. No picking her up from school or taking her on outings with just the two of you."

Keli raised her head, hope shining in her eyes.

When she looked like she was about to speak, I lifted a finger and she closed her mouth. "Monday, I have a meeting with a family law attorney. After I talk with him, we'll discuss how custody will be handled from here on out."

How she responded to my offer would determine how willing I would be to work with her on things. I would do everything in my power to prevent this from happening again, and I had the resources to do it. I hoped that she would understand that and take the opportunity she had been given.

"I understand. I'll make things right. With you and with Evanne."

After a moment, I nodded. "All right then. Let's go. I'm sure Evanne wants to sleep in her own bed tonight."

EIGHTEEN

LUMEN

"I'll call you when I know more," I promised Mai as she pulled up to the hospital. "Thanks for the ride."

"Of course," she said, her expression somber. "I hope she's okay."

"Me too."

I hurried through the hallways, following the directions Josalyn had given me fifteen minutes ago. She hadn't provided me with any details beyond saying that Soleil was in the hospital, and my presence when Josalyn saw her would be a big help, which meant when I stepped off the elevator, I was surprised to find myself at the psych ward.

"Lumen, over here," Josalyn called to me.

I hurried to where she stood, her face pinched with

worry. "What happened?" I had a feeling I knew, but I wasn't going to believe it until someone said it for sure.

"She tried to kill herself. One of the other kids found her and called 911."

"Dammit." Everything in me sank. "Will she be okay?"

"I haven't had the chance to talk to anyone yet. Brie called me from the ER, and by the time I got here, they'd already moved Soleil up here."

I looked around. "Where is Brie?"

"I sent her home. As you can imagine, the other kids are extremely upset. That's one of the reasons I called you. If we're able to see Soleil, I don't want her to think she's in trouble or that everyone is mad at her."

I nodded. That made sense.

Neither of us spoke as we waited, and I wondered if her mind was creating hundreds of different scenarios like mine was. If so, she was doing a better job of holding it in than I was. I couldn't stand still. Back and forth I paced, never going more than a few feet one way or another, afraid I'd miss something important if I wasn't right there when the doctor came out.

By the time the doctor approached us, I'd had to shove my hands into my pockets because I was so keyed up my fingers were trembling.

"Soleil Artz?"

"I'm Josalyn Brodie, her caseworker. This is Lumen Browne."

If he thought it strange that Josalyn didn't explain who I was, he didn't mention it. "How much did the ER doctor tell you?"

"She took all the painkillers she'd gotten yesterday, and one of the other foster kids found her just before she passed out. The ER pumped her stomach and gave her fluids, then sent her up here." Josalyn's tone was matter of fact, but I could see the little things that gave away how stressed she was. The wrinkles at the corners of her eyes. The way she held her clipboard almost like a shield.

"Correct. Considering what happened to her and that she'd just gotten the prescription, it was apparent that she tried to commit suicide. That's an automatic twenty-four-hour hold," the doctor explained.

"Are we able to see her?" Josalyn asked.

"She's sedated, but she might be aware enough to know that you're here. Follow me."

I WASN'T sure how common it was for a person to be allowed to sit with someone on a suicide hold, but after Josalyn took the head nurse aside for a quiet conversation, she came back and told me that I could stay with Soleil as long as I wanted. She stayed with me for a while, but after half an hour with Soleil still not having woken up, Josalyn decided her time would be better spent talking to Brie. With everything that had happened recently, the chances of Soleil not being moved were slim. It sucked, but Brie had other kids to think about.

I stayed.

I'd been there almost an hour when Soleil finally stirred. She coughed, breathing ragged, and I got up to call for a nurse. He came with water, and I stayed back while he did all the things he was supposed to do. Only after he left did I come forward, and Soleil saw me.

"What are you doing here?" The girl's voice was rough, her throat obviously raw.

"Because I'm worried about you," I said honestly and put my hand on hers. "A lot of people are. Josalyn was here when Brie first brought you in."

She closed her eyes, and for a moment, I thought she'd fallen asleep again.

"Who found me?"

I winced, wishing I wasn't the one who had to tell her this. I'd asked Josalyn before she left, though, just in case Soleil asked.

"Diana."

"Fuck." Soleil opened her eyes, and I saw the sheen of tears. "Kaitlyn's my roommate, so I thought it'd be her."

I pulled my chair closer to the bed and sat down. "You wanted Kaitlyn to be the one to find you?"

"I figured she could handle it." Soleil looked down at her arms. "No restraints?"

"I told them you wouldn't try anything if I was here," I said. "You can talk to me, you know. Let me help you."

Until meeting Soleil, I'd never realized how hard it was to do nothing. I wanted her to confide in me, tell me what happened so I could figure out how to fix it, or at least help her get through it. But she was quiet for several long minutes, and I thought we were back to where we'd been before, with her refusing to talk to me.

"My mom's boyfriend, Clyde, is a cop."

I froze, feeling like if I moved wrong, she'd close up again.

"We've been sneaking around for more than a year. That's why I thought I was pregnant before."

I couldn't breathe. I'd known when I'd bought the pregnancy test for Soleil that an adult might have been the potential father, but her mother's boyfriend, who also happened to be a cop? Fuck. My hands curled into fists. When I left here, I was going to find the son of a bitch and cut his fucking balls off.

"He didn't rape me," Soleil said quickly. "I wanted to do it."

"It doesn't matter if you wanted to," I explained gently. "You're underage, and he's an adult. A cop. He knows better."

She wiped the tears from her cheeks. "I never had no one want me except him. My mom's other boyfriends wanted her to get rid of me. They never wanted me around. Clyde wasn't like that. The three of us would go places, and he'd call us 'his girls.'"

I changed my mind. I wasn't going to simply cut his balls off. I was going to take everything and force it down his throat. That sounded much better than my original plan.

"After Mom went away, I snuck out to see him a couple times, and I kept waiting for him to tell me I could move in with him, but he didn't. I went to see him the day after I tried to steal that pregnancy test. I thought he loved me." Soleil's voice cracked, and new tears spilled down her cheeks.

"Oh, sweetie." I gave her hand a gentle squeeze.

"When I got to his place, I saw him with some woman. They were standing in front of his door, kissing."

I hated this man more with every passing second.

"Wednesday, I cut school to go see him. I wanted

him to explain why he was with her. Why he didn't want me anymore."

I really didn't want to hear what came next because I had a feeling this was what led to Soleil's condition when I'd found her in front of my door Thursday night.

"He told me it hadn't meant anything. Just like how my mom hadn't. He said he only wanted me. After..." She dashed away the tears and took a deep breath. "After we were done, I asked him if I could come live with him now. He asked how much I wanted it. I said I'd do anything, so he called some of his friends and said if I...if I made them happy, he'd think about it. I didn't want to. I told them no. They didn't care. And then he told them to dump me somewhere because he didn't want something...used."

"Fuck, Soleil..." I closed my eyes, attempting to block the pain of her words.

"Anyway, that's why I did it. Tried to off myself. Mom's in prison and probably doesn't give a damn about what happened to me. She never liked how much time Clyde spent with me. Probably say I deserved it. So, she don't want me and he don't want me. No one will after..." She shrugged, turning her face away from me. "What's left for me now?"

"I'm so sorry that happened to you. None of this is on you. It's on them. They're the ones who're wrong." I struggled to keep back my own tears. "You are an amazing young woman, and I promise you, there are people who love you unconditionally. You're not alone. I will help you get through this."

And I'd make that fucking bastard pay for what he did.

NINETEEN
ALEC

IN THE PAST, KELI HAD SENT ME PICTURES OF Evanne in her costumes and a couple pictures of her while trick-or-treating. I'd never been a part of the process.

It was quite entertaining, actually. Especially since Evanne hadn't been able to decide on just one costume when I'd taken her shopping yesterday. Now that Keli was here, Evanne insisted on modeling each costume for both of us and having us decide which one she should wear.

"Which one?" Evanne asked as she twirled, her shiny skirt billowing out around her. "Princess, cheetah, or ninja?"

"That's quite the range you have there, *mo chride*," I said with a chuckle.

"I have potential," she said. She was practically beaming. "Everybody says so."

Keli and I burst out laughing, the sound easing the tension between us. She'd been perfectly polite from the moment she'd gotten here, but I still didn't trust her. I doubted I'd ever completely trust her again. Still, she appeared to be making an effort at least.

"Well, do you feel more like a princess, a cheetah, or a ninja?" Keli asked.

Evanne screwed up her face in thought. "I feel more like an ogre."

"No surprise there." I chuckled. "Do you have an ogre costume?"

"No, but I can make mud and roll around in it. Then I'd look like an ogre no matter what I wear." Her eyes went wide, her face lighting up. "I could roll in mud and *then* wear the princess dress. I'd be Fiona from *Shrek*!"

I saw then that I needed to step in before Evanne acted on her idea and decided to go find or make mud. I loved her creativity, but there was a better way to prevent the enormous mess that particular costume would bring about.

"*Mo chride*, perhaps save that for next year. Then we can find appropriate makeup rather than rolling about in the mud." An idea came to me, and I said it before I could second guess myself. "If you want to combine costumes, you could add the princess tiara to the cheetah costume and be a cheetah princess."

Both Keli and Evanne stared at me, and I wondered if I'd made a father faux pa or if my suggestion was too far-fetched.

Then Evanne squealed and dove at me.

"That's perfect! Thank you!" She wiggled out of my embrace and ran for her room, shouting over her shoulder, "Come on, Mom! I need help with the makeup!"

Keli stood, but before she went, she said, "I know you sometimes worry about not being a good father, but that right there, that was great dad stuff."

Despite the issues between the two of us, I appreciated the reassurance and gave her a smile as she followed after Evanne. I stayed where I was. The idea might have been mine, but when it came to prep, anything more than buying a costume was beyond my skills. I'd leave that to Keli.

My doorbell rang, and I stood. It still was early for trick-or-treat, but I wouldn't turn any kids away. The years I'd worked on Halloween, I'd had my assistant, Tuesday, come to the house and hand out candy. She always joked that I preferred that to having to clean egg off my house or toilet paper off my trees, but we both knew it was more about the McCrae name. I didn't want my house or my family to be associated with a cold, rich miser who ignored his community. Having candy for kids once a year was a small thing.

Those were the thoughts going through my mind as I picked up the bowl of candy that sat next to the entrance and opened the door. My mind was so fixed on trick-or-treaters that it took me a moment to realize that it wasn't a kid standing in front of me.

"Lumen. You're here." I felt like an idiot stating the obvious that way, but I couldn't think of anything else to say.

"Can I come in?"

"Of course, please." I stepped to the side, and as she passed by me, I saw what I'd missed in my surprise before.

She looked like she'd been through, as the saying went, hell. Dark circles under her eyes. A pinched look to her face. Her hair was pulled back in a simple pony-tail, and her clothes were rumpled, as if she'd slept in them.

"Are you all right, lass?" I closed the door and waited for her to lead the way to the living room. "Not that I'm unhappy to see you, mind you. I've missed you."

I surprised myself with the admission, not because it was untrue, but because I'd offered it so quickly. If it surprised Lumen, however, it didn't show. She stopped just a few steps past me and turned around.

"Evanne will be happy—"

"I need to talk to your brother Eoin."

"—to see you." I finished the sentence even as my brain was processing what she'd said. "What?"

"I need to speak to Eoin," she repeated, her gaze everywhere but on me. "I didn't know if he was staying here or if you could tell me where he is. A phone number would work too."

I felt as if she was speaking a foreign language, as if I didn't have the ability to understand the actual words she was using. She wouldn't have come all the way here, after the way things had gone the last time we'd talked, only to ask about my brother. Nothing about Evanne. Nothing about what had happened between us. Just statements declaring her only interest here was Eoin.

When I didn't say anything right away, she crossed her arms and fixed her gaze on the floor, but didn't say a word. That annoyed me almost as much as what she wanted. I'd just told her that I missed her, and she hadn't responded. Aside from it being a blow to my pride, it proved that I had been right about her priorities.

"I think if Eoin wanted you to get in touch with him, he would have provided you with a number himself."

That earned me a glare. "What, exactly, are you accusing me of, Alec?

I responded to her question with one of my own. "Why do you want to speak to my brother?"

She lifted her chin, a stubborn set to her jaw, but I didn't get the chance to hear her answer because, at that moment, Evanne came running down the stairs, calling for me.

"Daddy! Where are you? I'm a cheetah princess!" She came into the hall at a run, nearly bowling Lumen over. "Ms. Browne!"

"Hey, kiddo." Lumen's smile was strained, but her affection for Evanne was genuine. "I like your costume."

"She's ready to go, Alec. We just..." Keli's voice trailed off as soon as she saw Lumen. "Ms. Browne. This is a surprise."

The words were polite, which I appreciated, but they didn't fool me. Keli was not happy at all about Lumen's presence, and she was more than a little suspicious of me regarding this surprise as well.

"Look at me! I'm a cheetah princess!" Evanne did a charming little pose that I would've found even more adorable if the current situation hadn't been so awkward.

"That you are." Lumen tapped Evanne's glittery tiara. "You make a lovely cheetah princess."

"We really should get going," Keli said, her voice as

frozen as her expression. "The weather's only supposed to be good for a few hours."

"Why don't you and Evanne get her candy bag?" I gave Keli a look that I hoped she could read.

"Sure thing. Come on, sweetie."

"Bye, Lumen!" Evanne hugged Lumen one more time before skipping after her mother.

"I'll be going too," Lumen said with a tight smile. "Once you give me what I came for."

"He's not here," I said bluntly. "And I won't be giving you personal information about my brother without his knowledge."

For a moment, I thought she'd argue with me, and I almost hoped for it. This wasn't like her. The being stubborn was, but the lack of passion in her voice was something new. I would rather have her angry and yelling at me than this flat affect.

"Fine. I'll ask Hob for help." With that, she shoved past me and walked out into the cool October evening.

"Things between you two aren't going well, are they?" Keli's tone was sympathetic. She put a hand on my arm. "Let her go. Without her, maybe things can be different with us."

I picked up Keli's hand and removed it from my arm. "Lumen isn't the reason you and I aren't going to be together. You're Evanne's mother, and I think we can be friends at some point, but that's all we'll ever be. We're not right together, and when you finally admit that, then you can move on too."

I didn't add that, sometimes, moving on wasn't all it was reported to be.

TWENTY

LUMEN

I didn't know what I was thinking, going to Alec's house to ask for him to put me in contact with his brother. The last two times Alec and I had been together, we'd fought, and we hadn't resolved any of the issues that had gotten us to that point in the first place. Why had I thought for even a moment that he'd put that aside to help me, or that he'd even care why I was asking, I didn't know. I knew how the world worked, how people really were. The only emotion he'd displayed had been jealousy, and I was willing to bet that was more due to wounded pride than anything else.

No matter how much I wished things were different.

He'd told me things with Keli were over, but she'd been there, looking as if she belonged within those walls. Sure, maybe she was just there so they could take

155

Evanne trick-or-treating together, but I didn't have much in the way of trust at the moment, not when it came to him.

The two people sitting on the sofa when I came into my apartment, however, I trusted completely. One look at my face, and Mai was up and coming toward me with arms wide.

"What happened?" she asked as she hugged me. "You left me a voicemail saying Soleil was at the hospital, and you'd tell me everything when you got home."

"She tried to kill herself," I said bluntly. "And she had a damn good reason."

Hob was on his feet. "Let me get you something to drink before you get into it." He headed toward the kitchen. "You want water or something stronger?"

"I think we could all use something stronger," I said, my shoulders slumping. "Trust me when I say you'll want it for what I have to tell you."

Hob just nodded and went to the fridge. Mai and I moved to the sofa, and when Hob joined us, we each took a long pull from the bottles in our hands. Mai and Hob didn't know yet what I knew, but Mai and I had been friends long enough that she was taking me seriously.

"Soleil's mom's bastard boyfriend groomed and raped her for more than a year. When she went missing earlier this week, she went to him because she thought he loved her. He used her, then gave her to some friends."

Mai and Hob started cursing under their breath after the first sentence and kept going as I talked.

"Take whatever you're imagining and make it worse. She talked about it in the hospital, but she won't talk to the cops about it. Just talking to me..." The anger that had fueled me before was gone, leaving only profound sadness. "She downed all of her painkillers yesterday. One of the other kids found her, and she's alive. I won't say she's okay, because after what happened to her, she's far from fucking okay. But she's alive."

I paused to finish my beer, and they did the same.

"I want to take down the assholes who assaulted her, including the mom's boyfriend." I took a breath and peeled the label from the bottle. "Thing is, he's a cop. And chances are, his gang-raping buddies are too."

Mai let loose with a torrent of English and Chinese curses. Hob simply set down his now empty beer, a hard look on his usually open face. He was a doctor, which meant he understood the sort of injuries Soleil must've had even without seeing her.

"What hospital was she taken to?" His voice was quiet.

I told him, and his expression tightened. "A guy I

went to med school with works in the ER over there. Whenever we have a particularly hard day, we'll meet up after our shifts are done. Friday morning, he texted me, asking if I was free for breakfast. He had this kid who'd come in, beaten and assaulted, and she wouldn't tell anyone what'd happened to her."

I rubbed at the pain forming in my temple. "Shit."

"Yeah." Hob's eyes glinted with anger. "This guy was a medic in the army right out of high school, so it's not like he hasn't seen his fair share of fucked up stuff, but this one..." He shook his head. "It really had him shaken up."

"Did she tell anyone other than you?" Mai asked.

"I don't think so," I said. "Brie and Josalyn would have a legal obligation to report it, and Soleil is terrified."

"No shit." Mai stood up and took our empty bottles into the kitchen. A minute later, she was back with three more. "I'd be scared too if the person who'd hurt me was someone who was supposed to protect me."

"That's a part of it," I agreed. "The worst part, though, is that she still wants to believe that he cares about her. Even if I decided to go to the police about it, it'd be hearsay, and she'd never corroborate it. And if the rape kit doesn't pick up his DNA..." I shrugged, feeling completely hopeless.

"If you're not going to the cops, what are you going to do?"

Mai knew me well. There was no way I'd simply sit on this information and not try to figure out a way to help. Right now, Soleil was my main focus, but I knew that there was a good chance she wasn't the first one he'd done this to. And if this man wasn't stopped, she wouldn't be the last.

What too many people didn't understand was that, unlike murderers, sex offenders were hardly ever singular offenders. A man who killed his wife in a fit of rage or a drunk driver who killed someone wouldn't necessarily do it again. And even multiple murderers, like gang members, could walk away from those circumstances and never hurt anyone again. Sex offenders were almost always repeat offenders, especially if they weren't caught. And they sometimes would escalate to murder to prevent their victims from reporting them.

I was fairly certain that's what the bastard had intended to happen to Soleil when he'd given her to his friends. He'd counted on her either dying or being so traumatized that she'd never tell anyone what had happened to her.

The one thing he hadn't factored into his plan was me. I didn't give a damn if he threatened me, and I wouldn't be intimidated by him.

"I want to take him down," I said. "It took me a couple hours, but I was able to find his name. Clyde Lunsford. That's the son of a bitch who preyed on her. Him first, then his buddies."

"I would ask if you're crazy, but I already know the answer to that question," Mai said grimly. "The real question is, are you going to let us help?"

Hope swelled in my chest. "I was hoping you'd offer. As much as I hate the idea of bringing you into all of this, I know I can't do it by myself."

"We're in," Hob said. "What is it you want us to do?"

"That's just it." I held up both hands, feeling helpless. "I don't have a plan. All I've really been able to think about is how I can castrate all of them."

"That would most likely land you in jail, and you couldn't do anything from there," Mai said, an angry smile curving her lips. "But I agree with the sentiment."

"As uncomfortable as the idea of castration makes me, in this case, I tend to agree." Hob shifted in his seat, crossing his legs. "But Mai's right. Assaulting any of them, no matter how much they deserve it, won't solve any problems. We need a way to get this Lunsford guy to either confess to what he's done or catch him trying to do something else."

While a part of me still wished I had someone like Eoin in on this – I loved Hob, but Eoin was a hell of a lot scarier – I was grateful to have my friends with me. I'd told Soleil that she didn't have to do everything on her own, and it was a lesson I was still learning myself. As we began to pitch ideas, I was glad I'd reached out. One way or another, we'd figure something out to get Soleil some justice and keep those men from hurting anyone else.

TWENTY-ONE
LUMEN

WHILE THE OTHER KIDS KEPT THEMSELVES BUSY with their math worksheets, I called Evanne up to my desk so we could go over what she'd missed the previous week. As she skipped up to the desk I kept next to mine specifically for instances like this, I was relieved to see that she didn't seem to have been negatively affected by what had happened.

"You and I are going to talk about the lessons you missed last week," I began. "Anything that you don't understand, you need to ask about, because I won't know how to help otherwise."

"I'm glad to be back," Evanne said as she squirmed in her chair. "Mommy and I had fun, but I don't like missing school."

"Well, we missed you too." I wasn't sure if that

sounded sincere or lame, but it was all I had to go with at the moment. "How about we start with the spelling test you missed?"

"I studied yesterday before I went trick-or-treating." She pulled out a piece of paper and a pencil. "I'm ready."

I couldn't help but smile. "Very good. Number one..."

We went through the list rather quickly since she didn't need me to repeat any of the words, and then I said I'd give her a minute before we moved on to language arts.

"I got lots of candy last night." Evanne patted her tummy for emphasis. "And everyone liked my cheetah princess costume."

I grinned at her. She had been adorable. "It was a good costume."

"Daddy came up with the idea."

That was a surprise. "Did he now?"

"Mm-hm. And Mommy took pictures." She took out her language arts book and opened it to the last lesson we'd done. "I promised Uncle Brody and Uncle Eoin pictures."

As much as I'd promised myself I'd keep things professional, however, I couldn't resist the opportunity that had just presented itself. "Did your mom send the picture to them, or did she send it to your dad?"

Okay, not over the line, but still toeing it. Then again, I'd dated – or was dating? – her dad, so it wasn't too weird a question to ask.

"Mom sent it to my phone so I could send it to my uncles. They don't really like each other."

That wasn't a surprise.

"Do you send a lot of messages to your uncles?" I hoped I sounded casual rather than creepy because creepy was the last way a third-grade teacher should sound.

Evanne nodded. "Uncle Eoin was a soldier since before I was born. Daddy gave me a phone so Uncle Eoin and I could send pictures and messages to each other while he was gone."

"He was a soldier?" That explained a lot. The way he carried himself. The authority in his voice.

His scar.

"Yeah. Then he got hurt and came home. He lives with Grand-da and Grandma now."

I wanted to ask more, but I couldn't justify continuing a conversation about her uncle when she had work to get through. I turned our attention to language arts and promised myself I'd only come back to the conversation if the opportunity presented itself.

On our way back from lunch a couple hours later, that's exactly what happened. We stopped at the restroom, and Evanne was at the head of the line, which meant she was the first one finished and stood next to me while we waited for the others.

"Do you think I could ask Uncle Eoin to come in for show and tell some time? He could talk about being in the army."

I wasn't entirely sure bringing someone as scary looking as Eoin into an elementary classroom was a good idea, but he seemed to do well with Evanne, so maybe it could work. To find out, I'd need to talk to him, though. And to do *that*, I needed a way to contact him.

"That might be possible." I chewed my bottom lip. "You wouldn't happen to have your phone with you today, would you? I don't have your uncle's phone number."

"I don't bring my phone to school," she said seriously. "Daddy says I have to leave it at home."

It was on the tip of my tongue to ask her to bring it tomorrow, just so I didn't have to ask whichever of her parents came to pick her up, but she lifted her finger, her face brightening.

"But I can give you Uncle Eoin's phone number. Daddy made me memorize all of my aunts' and uncles' phone numbers in case I had an emergency. Grand-da's and Grandma's numbers too."

My eyebrows went up. "That's pretty impressive. Most people, myself included, don't bother since our phones store them."

"Daddy says it's better to have them memorized because we never know when our phones may break or our batteries die."

"Your dad is a very smart man." I wished I'd been able to say that with less of a twinge, but at least I'd managed to get it out without my feelings leaking into my words.

"I know. I get it from him."

I was saved from having to stifle a laugh when a pair of squabbling boys came out of the bathroom, each blaming the other for splashing water. By the time I got back to Evanne, she'd moved on to a different subject, but not one I found any less interesting...though it was far more confusing.

"I think you should come to dinner again. Daddy likes you better than he likes Mommy."

Dammit.

This was not a conversation I wanted to have. "We'll have to see what your dad thinks about that."

Let him be the one to tell his daughter about whatever he and I were or weren't.

TWENTY-TWO
ALEC

My meeting with Percival this morning had gone well. I liked the way he worked. He'd done as he'd promised and put together several different custody agreements. When we'd gone over them, he'd offered his opinion on each one but hadn't tried to persuade me one way or the other.

Each of the options had merit.

One granted me sole custody with Keli only having DCFS supervised visits.

The second granted me sole custody and gave me full control over when Keli's visits were and how long they lasted.

The third was an agreement where I had primary custody, and Keli had a set schedule of every other weekend and every other holiday for visitation.

The final one was a more traditional joint custody agreement with Evanne going back and forth every other week or month

I hadn't made a definite decision yet. I wanted to watch Keli a little while longer, see how she handled things now that she and Evanne were back in Seattle. The last one wouldn't be a possibility at any point in the near future. I also didn't want to do the first unless she did something crazy. Which meant I was debating between the middle two options.

It wasn't, however, thoughts of the custody issue that were distracting me from the email I'd been trying to write for the past fifteen minutes. It was the same thing that had been circling in my head since last night.

I had royally fucked up with Lumen.

To make things right, I needed to speak to her. I had acted rashly more than once when it came to her. She made me behave erratically, impulsively. For her to know the things I needed her to know, I had to explain. Think rationally. Plan out each point I would make and the words I would use. She would understand the choices I'd made, the reasons why I'd made them.

Now that things with Keli and Evanne had settled down, Lumen and I could move past our disagreement and put all of it behind us.

Except my gut said that she wouldn't be open to

discussing anything unless I was willing to admit I had been in the wrong. But I hadn't been. Evanne was my number one priority, and she would always be my number one priority.

The frustration I felt at not being able to see a solution grew as my day continued. I was unaccustomed to not being able to find answers, to fix problems. I accomplished whatever I put my mind to, and I always had. I refused to believe that I couldn't do the same here.

I finally managed to finish my email and sent it off. When I glanced at the clock on the top right of my computer screen, I saw it was close to one. I didn't have a lunch meeting, which meant I could stay in and eat here, catch up on additional work. Or I could take a break and go somewhere nice.

Before I could decide, Tuesday buzzed my intercom. "Sir, your brother's here."

"Send him in," I said. I assumed it was Eoin, and a few seconds later, I saw that I was right. "You know I planned on telling the family how things went with the lawyer. You didn't want to wait?"

"I'm actually not here about that," he said as he took the seat across from me. "Not that I'd argue if you wanted to give me a head's up since I'm here."

"It went well. I'm deciding between two agreements, and once I do, I'll take it to Keli and see what the next step will be." I leaned back in my chair and linked my hands. "Now, how about you tell me why you came by since it isn't about my custody meeting."

"I came because your girlfriend or your ex-girlfriend – whatever Lumen Browne is to you – called me about an hour ago." He paused, studying me for several seconds before continuing. "She wants my help with something."

I scowled. "If it's to get me to apologize for putting Evanne first, you're wasting your time."

"Actually, she didn't mention you at all."

I frowned. "All right. Whatever message you're supposed to pass along, say it. I have work to do."

"I know you've had a bad couple weeks, but that's no excuse for being an asshat," he said mildly. "I'm not here on her behalf. In fact, I have a feeling she'd be pissed at me if she knew I was here."

"Then why are you here, Eoin?" I asked, irritated. "You clearly think something is important enough to interrupt me at work, so please, tell me what it is."

He raised an eyebrow, and I suddenly felt as if he was the elder brother, about to chastise me for misbehaving.

"There's a girl, a foster kid named Soleil–"

"I know who she is," I interrupted. "She went

missing the same day Evanne did. Lumen and I fought about it because she prioritized the girl over Evanne."

"The more you try to make Lumen the bad guy here, the worse you're going to feel when you finally let me finish what I'm saying."

I glared at him but waved a hand for him to continue.

"Soleil did run away." He held up a finger, stopping me before I could even take a breath to argue. "She went to see her mother's boyfriend, a forty-something cop who'd convinced her that it was okay for the two of them to have sex even though she was only thirteen when it started."

My stomach churned, guilt slamming into me hard enough to take my breath away. As Eoin continued to explain what had happened, it became difficult to breathe. I felt like I was suffocating. I didn't consider myself a naïve person, but I hadn't even considered the possibility that this girl had been assaulted, much less in that way.

"That's where I come in," Eoin said. "Lumen wants me to help her and her friends set up this cop, make it so he'll be off the streets without Soleil having to go through a trial."

The silence that settled between us was thick, and even though Eoin didn't reiterate his opinion of my behavior, the weight of his gaze was enough to let me know the low opinion he had of me at the moment.

"She came to see me yesterday, asking how to get in touch with you," I admitted. "I refused to tell her. I said it was because I didn't want to give out your personal information, but that was a lie. I was jealous."

"You're an idiot."

"Aye." I barked out a soft laugh. "That I am."

He sighed. "Look, I'm not good when it comes to talking about feelings and emotions. Neither of us are. But I do have some advice." He leaned forward. "Get your head out of your ass and go to her."

"Do you think it would do any good?" I asked, the sick feeling in my stomach growing. "Wouldn't it be too little, too late?"

"I don't know," he said. "But one thing is for certain. If you don't at least try to apologize, you'll have lost her for good."

He had a point.

I raked all ten fingers through my hair, frustrated to the core. "I don't like being wrong."

To my surprise, Eoin laughed. "No shit. You're the same kid who used to lock himself in his room whenever someone was able to prove something you said was wrong. You're also one of the most stubborn people I've ever met, and that's a dangerous combination."

"Nice to know what you really think of me," I said dryly.

"As if those are personality traits you're not already aware of."

"That is true."

"You haven't changed much from when you were a kid," he said. "I guess the question now is, what are you willing to do if it means salvaging what you and Lumen have?"

Just as I was about to say that I didn't know, the real answer came through, clear as anything. It had always been there too. I just hadn't allowed myself to see it.

I pushed the intercom button on my phone. "Tuesday, reschedule all of my appointments for the rest of the day. I'm leaving."

TWENTY-THREE
LUMEN

School today had been nice and boring. I followed my lesson plan exactly, and we'd had no drills or surprises. Just our normal schedule and basic lessons. The kids hadn't been exceptionally good or exceptionally bad, just normal kids. A little talking, a little noise, but otherwise, good behavior.

After everything that had happened recently, it had been nice to focus solely on teaching. This was what I'd gone to school for, what I'd always wanted to do. It was nice to finally feel like I was finally getting the opportunity to prove myself.

It wasn't until the final bell had rung, and my last student had gone that I got a text from Josalyn. Soleil was being released today, and Josalyn wanted me to be there. Brie wouldn't be off work until later this evening, and Josalyn thought it would be better if she and I picked Soleil up and took her home as soon as she was allowed to leave rather than making her wait.

So, instead of heading home to relax with some dinner and TV, I was on my way to the hospital. Again. While I had no regrets about my promise to be there for Soleil, I hoped it would be the last time I needed to go to the hospital for a while.

Josalyn was already in Soleil's room by the time I arrived, the caseworker going over some papers with a doctor while the patient stared off into space. I would have thought she was simply being a sullen, uncommunicative teenager if I hadn't seen the way her hands were gripping the hospital blanket.

She was petrified.

After what she told me, I didn't blame her.

I wanted to tell her that everything would be okay. That I had a plan to make her safe and to make Clyde pay. But I knew I couldn't really promise her anything. There were too many things that could possibly go wrong. Giving her hope only to take it away would be worse than not doing anything at all.

Still, she needed to know that she was safe.

"Hey, ready to get out of here?" I smiled at her as I crossed to her bed. "Looks like Josalyn is doing the heavy lifting with the paperwork. Do you need me to get you anything?"

Soleil shook her head but didn't look at me. Since she'd told me what had happened, she hadn't made eye contact with me. I wanted to tell her that she had no reason to be embarrassed or ashamed. Nothing that had happened to her was her fault. Even running away had come about due to Clyde's manipulation.

"You have clothes to change into?"

She pointed to a bag at the foot of the bed.

"All right, then let's get you dressed." I picked up the bag and held it out to her. "I'm guessing you can handle that by yourself?"

I got an eyeroll, which was at least something.

"All right," Josalyn said as the doctor left. "He'll send someone back with a wheelchair, so let's get you dressed and ready to go."

Soleil picked up her bag and limped into the bathroom without a word. As the door closed behind her, Josalyn turned to me, concern on her face.

"She still isn't talking about it?" I asked.

Josalyn shook her head. "She refuses to talk to the psychologist other than to say that she'd made a mistake in trying to kill herself. She agreed to go to counseling. That's as far as I've gotten with her. You're still the only one she's told."

I'd told Josalyn that Soleil had talked to me, but not the content of the conversation. I'd expected Josalyn to be upset when I'd refused to tell her everything, but she'd said to tell her only what was necessary. I'd told her to keep everyone from Soleil's past away from her. That had been enough.

For now.

"I'll keep talking to her," I promised.

"You do that," Josalyn said. "Because I don't think she'll get through this alone."

The bathroom door opened before I could respond. Soleil came out looking more comfortable in jeans and a hoodie, but she moved as if she was afraid she'd break at the slightest touch. I couldn't even imagine how emotionally and physically fragile she felt right now. To my surprise, she didn't argue as she sat down in the wheelchair the nurse had provided.

Josalyn had driven, which meant we didn't have to take a cab. It also meant we could let Soleil sit in the back by herself and not feel like we were crowding her. She hadn't said anything to me about going back to the group home after what had happened, but I was sure it was on her mind. I didn't see how it couldn't be.

"You don't have to come in with me," Soleil said as Josalyn pulled into the driveway. "I know where my room is."

"Too bad," I said cheerfully. "I want to see everyone."

"I need to give Brie some paperwork," Josalyn added.

"Whatever," Soleil muttered. She got out of the car.

"Do you think she'll ever be willing to talk to the police about what happened?" Josalyn asked.

I weighed the question carefully before answering as honestly as I could. "Probably not, but she could surprise me."

Josalyn nodded grimly, and we made our way to the house together.

Brie wasn't back yet, but the kids were all home from school. I heard Diana yell her friend's name as Josalyn and I walked up the stairs to the front door. By the time I stepped inside, Diana had Soleil in a bear hug, and Lakeith was patting Soleil's shoulder as if he wasn't entirely sure how to show her that he was glad she was back.

"Hey, kiddo." Soleil's voice was hoarse. "I'm so sorry you had to see that. I didn't mean...I'm just sorry."

"I'm glad you're okay." Diana bounced back. "But don't do it again, okay? It was scary."

"Okay. I promise."

That appeared to be enough for Diana because she switched from Soleil to me. "Lumen!"

I hugged Diana even as I watched Soleil climb the stairs, one painful step at a time. I almost excused myself to go after her, but then I saw Kaitlyn following her. Kaitlyn Parsons was the last person I would've thought of as helpful, but a glimpse of her face as she went made me think that I might have misjudged her.

I'd stay until Brie arrived, just in case Soleil needed me, but I wouldn't push. If Kaitlyn could get Soleil talking, all the better. Having a friend her age to support her would be a good thing. And that left me free to deal with Clyde and his bastard friends.

I'D FORGOTTEN what a great cook Brie was. With such a large group to feed, it would've been easier to use mass-produced processed foods. Hell, it was what most people ate anyway. Brie, however, made sure she always had at least one part of the meal made from scratch, and usually more than one.

Tonight's dinner had been one of her best. Spaghetti with her special sauce, meatballs from an old family recipe, garlic bread, and peach cobbler for dessert. Judging by the look on Soleil's face, it was her favorite meal.

The kids had been good with her when she'd come

down for dinner. I'd been a little worried since teenagers weren't exactly known for being kind or tactful, but they'd done well. No one had treated her any differently than they had any other time I'd seen them all together. Dinner was a raucous affair, filled with laughter and yelling, the sort of normal that would do Soleil's spirit as much good as the food would do her body.

I was actually in decent spirits as I left, confident that Brie and the kids could take care of Soleil while I worked on my plan to take down every person who'd hurt her.

Possibilities were still running through my head when I stepped onto my floor and saw someone sitting outside my door.

Again.

Except this time, it wasn't a scared and beaten teenage girl.

It was Alec.

TWENTY-FOUR
ALEC

THE MOMENT I SAW LUMEN, I SCRAMBLED TO MY feet. I'd been sitting in the hallway long enough that my ass was numb, but that didn't matter even a fraction as much as setting things right.

"What are you doing here?"

Under any other circumstances, that question would've been rude, but she sounded so tired that it only made me feel worse about how I'd behaved. I would do things differently this time...if she let me. The fear that she might just tell me to leave was very real.

"I was a right bastard to you, and I am sorrier for that than I can ever say." The words came out without thought, and I realized that it was probably a good thing. When I thought too much, I fucked things up.

She sighed, such a weary sound that I automatically

took a step forward before realizing that my touch might be unwanted.

"May I take your bag?" I held out my hand.

She handed it over and then dug into her purse for her keys. When she didn't take her bag back from me or shut the door behind her, I followed her inside. Neither of us said anything as we took off our shoes and coats, the atmosphere filled with the sort of tension that would explode with the slightest spark. Whether it would be for good or for bad still remained to be seen.

"I need a drink," she said. "Want one? It's not top shelf or anything, but it's beer, and it's cold."

"That would be great, thank you." I stayed standing, unsure and off-balance for the first time in my life. I didn't know where to go or what to do. This wasn't a problem I could solve through sheer willpower.

When she came back with two bottles of beer, she held one out to me and pointed to a chair. "Sit. I've been on my feet most of the day."

She sat on the couch, so I opted for the chair, not wanting her to think I was simply here for sex. I desperately wanted to touch her, but I wanted more than her body. Falling back on the physical chemistry between us would only make things worse.

"I understand if you never want to see me again," I

started, "but I owe you an apology. More than one. Perhaps some groveling as well."

Not even a hint of a smile.

"Eoin came to see me," I continued. "He told me why you'd wanted to talk to him."

She closed her eyes and rubbed her forehead as if she had a headache. "I wish he hadn't done that, but I can't say I'm really surprised. I hadn't told him to keep it from you because I honestly didn't think you'd care."

I winced. "I deserve that. I've been completely self-absorbed, deciding that my problems were more important than anyone else's. That my priorities were the only right ones."

"Evanne should be your first priority," Lumen said quietly. "I never meant for you to put anyone else ahead of her. I care about her a great deal."

"I know, and if I'd bothered to truly listen to you, I would have acknowledged it then. I had tunnel vision and refused to accept that anything or anyone could be more important than what I wanted." I leaned forward, my elbows on my knees. "I am truly and sincerely sorry."

She took a long draught of her beer before looking at me. "Thank you. And I'm sorry that I didn't help matters much by responding the way I did. Just like I can't know what it's like to be a parent, I shouldn't have expected you to understand my urgency about finding Soleil."

Without knowing it, Lumen had just led into the next apology I needed to make.

"What I said about family...I can't even tell you how sorry I am. It was wrong of me to lash out like that." With a deep breath, I let down the walls I always kept in place. She needed to know this wasn't simply lip service. "I have family baggage – not even close to what you've been through – but it affects me more than I care to admit."

She set down her half-empty bottle and turned toward me, her expression wary. The fact that she had yet to demand I leave gave me hope that what had broken between us wasn't beyond repair.

"I love my family, and I ken well how fortunate I am, but losing my mother when I did, then the Carideo family joining with ours and our move to America, it left its mark. I've never wanted to talk about it. Not then and not since then." I had made a decision on my way over here, and I would keep it no matter what happened between Lumen and me, but I hoped it would show her how serious I was about changing. "First thing tomorrow, I'll be finding a therapist. I cannae be the father Evanne deserves if I haven't worked through my own issues."

A small smile curved Lumen's lips. "I'm glad to hear that."

Encouraged, I took a deep breath. "I want to be

better for my daughter, but I also want to be better for you. I've fallen in love with you, lass, and I ken you deserve so much more than I have to offer, but I am willing to give you all I have. I cannae promise I'll never do something wrong again, but I can promise that I will work every day at becoming the man both you and Evanne deserve."

"You're in love with me?" Lumen's expression was unreadable, but her entire body had gone stiff.

"Aye, lass." I reached out and took her hand, holding it loosely enough that she could pull away if she wanted. "I love you, and I will do whatever you need me to do to make up for how I've acted these last few days. Give me a chance, please."

And then I stopped talking. It was all in her hands now. Whatever she decided, I would honor, even if it broke my heart.

I had always thought I was someone who didn't need love or even want it, but I saw now that way of thinking was only another shield I'd put into place to protect myself. How could I know what I was missing if I'd never had it to start?

Now that I knew what it was like to be in love, I never wanted to be without it. Without her. I could only wait and pray that she felt the same way about me and was willing to try again.

TWENTY-FIVE

LUMEN

Alec was in love with me.

More than that, he'd actually said *I love you*. Some people might not make a distinction between the two, but I got the feeling that Alec wasn't one of them. It hadn't been some emotional outburst. For someone who was as particular as he was, I imagined he'd spent his time sitting in my hallway, carefully planning exactly what he wanted to say.

Which meant he'd not only *said* those three little words, but he'd *wanted* to say them. He'd thought them through.

That wasn't the only thing he'd said that I was still processing. He was taking responsibility, acknowledging the root issues, and had a real plan in place to work on it. Therapy. Alec wouldn't lie about something like that.

The fact that he was going to talk to a professional was huge. Guys like him, they didn't usually go for things like that.

I believed him about all of it. But that was only the first step. The next one was all on me. I had to decide if I was willing to risk my heart. And it would be a risk because it was love. I couldn't deny it or pretend it wasn't true. I loved him too.

And it was time for me to stop hiding.

I got up and moved over to where he was sitting. He tilted his head back so that he was looking up at me, the expression on his face so raw that it confirmed everything I was feeling.

"I want that second chance too."

The relief on his face spoke volumes. I ran my fingers through his hair, and he leaned into my touch.

"I'm sorry for my part in what happened." My fingertips traced along his cheekbone and then moved to his jaw, stubble rough against my skin. "We both know I have my own baggage about family. I'm better than I used to be, but with Soleil..." My voice caught in my throat. "It was just too much. I got overwhelmed. I know better, but what happened to her..." I wasn't able to finish.

"It's all right, lass." He put his hands on my waist, his thumbs sliding under the hem of my shirt, brushing back and forth across my skin in a motion that managed to be both soothing and sensual at the same time. "We just need to get to know each other. Be aware of the things we struggle with. Talk to each other instead of yelling. Communicate."

"Now you're just showing off," I teased. I cupped his face in my hands and bent enough to brush my lips across his. "And, by the way, I love you too."

As soon as the words were out of my mouth, he was kissing me. He stood, sweeping me up in his arms so we didn't have to break the kiss. A few seconds later, we were in my room, and he was kicking the door shut behind us. We tumbled onto the bed, limbs tangled, far too many clothes between us. I tugged at his shirt, eager for skin on skin.

Suddenly, Alec caught my hands, stilling them. He raised himself up far enough for our eyes to meet.

"Are you certain this is what you want?" he asked. "I don't want to start our second chance with a mistake."

The sincerity on his face made my answer an easy one.

"I want this." I unbuttoned his shirt as I spoke. "I want *you*. I think this is the perfect way for us to celebrate our new start." I stopped with one button left. "Unless *you* don't want this."

His eyebrows shot up. He took one of my hands and

moved it down his body until I could feel the hard length of him straining against his zipper. "*Mo nighean bhan,* this is what you do to me with a single kiss."

I gave him a gentle squeeze. "Now that we've established that we're both willing and able..."

Alec rose up on his knees and pulled off his shirt, the last button easily coming free. He tossed the shirt aside, and I drank in the sight of him. A chuckle caught my attention, and I ran my gaze back up to his face. A smile on those kissable lips. Eyes dark and pupils wide.

"Your turn, lass."

I barely had time to get my shirt off before he was there, mouth on the side of my throat, hands sliding up my sides, leaving heat trailing after them. I tipped my head back to give him better access to my neck and ran my fingers over his broad shoulders, enjoying the feel of him.

My legs came up on either side of his waist, my skirt rucking up around my waist. His weight settled on me, the hard press of his cock behind his zipper now in the perfect position to put pressure on the suddenly damp crotch of my panties.

I moaned as his mouth moved lower, across my collarbone, and then down between my breasts. My nails dug into his skin, and he turned his head, biting the side of my breast. I gasped, my body jerking. He chuckled, the vibration sending a shiver through me.

He rolled his hips, sending a wave of pleasure rolling through me. The sound I made would have embarrassed me if I hadn't been trying to grind against him for more friction. Then his mouth latched onto one of my nipples, and I forgot to worry about being quiet. He sucked on the sensitive skin, tongue rubbing against the tip even as he continued rocking against me.

My orgasm came out of nowhere, exploding inside me with enough force to make every muscle in my body tense and white spots burst in front of my eyes. The world grayed out as I went limp, and I was dimly aware that Alec was moving away from me, but I didn't think I was up to protesting just yet. My brain and mouth weren't connecting well at this point. I let my mind drift until the mattress dipped next to me.

"I'll take it as a compliment that I could get you to come like that." He sounded smug, but it was well-deserved.

I smiled at him and echoed his words. "Your turn."

"I was hoping you'd say that." He shifted so that he could reach the waistband of my skirt. "May I?"

"I think you earned it." I winked at him.

He peeled off my skirt and took my panties with it.

"I fully intend to do wicked things to you with my tongue, but that will wait. I need to be inside you."

I saw now that, at some point between undressing himself completely and joining me on the bed again, he'd put on a condom. I parted my legs and held out a hand, just as eager to have him inside me as he was.

"Roll over."

I did as he said, trusting that whatever he had in store would be equally good for me as it would be for him.

"On your knees."

I repositioned my arms and legs underneath me, but instead of taking me, he gave yet another command.

"Up."

I straightened, and he wrapped one arm around my waist, pulling me back against him. His cock was hot against my ass, and I shivered in anticipation. I let him move me until I was right where he wanted me, and then he was sliding between my legs, latex smooth against my sensitive skin.

"Look." He turned my face so that I was looking directly in front of us.

At us.

I'd never noticed that the mirror I'd hung was in a perfect place to capture the reflection of what was happening in my bed. I'd never been particularly shy about my body, but walking by a mirror or trying on clothes was a completely different experience than staring at myself, skin flushed, nipples hard points. And then there was Alec. My body hid some of his, but he still took my breath away.

"I want you to watch us, *mo luaidh*."

"What does that one mean?" I asked, my eyes meeting his in the mirror.

"*My beloved. My darling.*" He moved my hair aside and kissed the side of my neck.

I turned my head, bringing our lips together. The arm around my waist tightened as he teased the seam of my mouth with his tongue. I opened for him, and the kiss deepened. Every place where his skin touched mine hummed with energy. When he broke the kiss, I frowned, trying to twist around, but he held me tight.

"Watch."

I turned my gaze back to the mirror and watched as he slid inside me. A shudder went through me from head to toe. When our bodies were finally flush against each other, he went still, his eyes locking with mine. I saw so much there, things he'd never let me see before. The love with the desire. The vulnerability behind the strength. The insecurity hidden by outward confidence.

I raised my arm behind me, fingers finding the short, soft hairs at the base of his skull. He moved the arm around my waist until one large hand covered a breast and his other hand was down between my legs. I drew in a shaking breath as a single-digit slid over my clit in a feather-light caress, too much and too little at the same time.

With excruciating slowness, he pulled back until only the tip of him was still in me. Then he moved forward at the same leisurely pace, letting me feel every inch of him. The strokes over my clit were just as maddening, enough to keep me going but not fast enough to trigger a climax. I tried to push against him, but his grip on me only tightened. Bit by bit, the fire inside me grew steadily bigger, flames licking across nerves and cells until the sensations consumed me.

"Look at yourself, lass. I love how you look when you give yourself over to me. So beautiful, *mhurninn*."

The words rolled over me, like silk against my skin. Seeing the heat in his eyes only bolstered them. These weren't meaningless platitudes. He meant everything he said.

"Come for me, lass. I want you to see what you look like when you come. When *I* make you come."

He shifted our position, leaning me forward just enough to change the angle. This time, when he pushed back inside, the entire length of his cock rubbed against my g-spot.

"Fuck!" I struggled to keep my eyes open, my attention on our reflections.

"Aye, that's it, lass. You're close." His fingers pressed more firmly on my clit.

I came again, crying out his name. This time, however, he didn't let me down gently. Instead, he drove into me hard and fast. The wave of pleasure I was riding crested higher, turning words into meaningless sounds. Every thrust took me to new heights, the intensity growing until I didn't think I could take anymore. My legs gave out at some point, and he held me up, his mouth pressed against my ear. His accent was almost too thick for me to understand the words, but the meaning was clear.

I was his.

With a shout, he buried himself deep enough to send small sparks of pain across my nerves, but they only added to everything else I felt. Every single sense was on high alert, taking in more information than my brain could process.

Salt on my lips from where I'd tasted his skin. His breathing hot and ragged, both felt and heard. The spicy, masculine scent of him. Sweat-slicked bodies, both mine and his. The raw, open emotion on our faces. I'd never felt so much before, and certainly not all at the same time.

We collapsed onto the bed in a tangled heap, both spent but satisfied. The real world would come crowding back in soon enough, but for right now, it was the two of us, right where we were supposed to be.

For the first time in weeks, I felt fully relaxed, and sleep came as no surprise. I was safe with him.

TWENTY-SIX
ALEC

Lumen and Evanne had their heads bent over a paper, both of them smiling and laughing about whatever it was they were reading. I'd just finished cleaning up our dinner mess and now stood in the doorway, watching the two of them.

I could get used to this.

The thought surprised me, but not as much as it would have a week ago. Since Lumen and I had worked things out a few days ago, we'd made purposeful steps toward building a healthy relationship. The first had been telling the people in our lives that we were together in order to prevent any unpleasant surprises.

Evanne had been thrilled since she'd been worrying about Lumen not having been around recently. Keli had been disappointed, but she'd handled it better than I'd anticipated. In fact, she'd been amenable to most things this past week, including looking on her own for an apartment.

I fully intended to continue paying child support, even though I now had primary custody of Evanne. Keli had come to depend on me doing things for her, and because I liked to be in control, I'd gone along with it. Not any longer.

Everything that had happened between us from the moment she'd dropped Evanne off and left for Italy was because she'd lost sight of who she was and what her life could be apart from being a mother. If I had paid a little more attention, I might have seen it before it had gotten this bad, but as they said, hindsight was twenty-twenty. We couldn't go back, only move forward.

And my forward was with the pair sitting at my kitchen table.

We did still have one more thing we needed to do before we could truly focus on what we wanted to build together, but that was set for tomorrow. Lumen had brought me in to the plan that she, Eoin, Hob, and Mai had created to stop the police officer who had assaulted Soleil. I didn't like it, but there didn't seem to be another way to go about this.

At least with Eoin there, I was fairly confident that he and I could keep the others safe. He was also supposed to talk to Brody about helping too. We'd all agreed that bringing another of my brothers along would be wise since we had no idea how things with Clyde would play out. A man who could do what he'd done was capable of anything.

Once Evanne was finished with her homework, we all settled in to watch one of Evanne's favorite Pixar movies. She sat between Lumen and me, happily wedged into a space that allowed her to snuggle against both of us.

If I hadn't seen the movie half a dozen times, I wouldn't have known a single plot point by the time it was done. My attention had been solely on the pair next to me. I felt as if I'd somehow tricked the universe into giving me far more than I ever could deserve. A wonderful woman and an equally wonderful daughter. A family I was only now realizing how much I'd taken for granted.

No more.

I would still work hard and refuse to compromise on quality, but MIRI would no longer be the center of my life. It would be Evanne and Lumen who would make up that core. My rational mind said that Lumen and I were still new in our relationship, but my intuition rarely steered me wrong, and it said she was the one.

This time, I planned to listen.

When the credits began, Evanne looked up at me, her hopeful expression alerting me to what would come next. She didn't disappoint.

"Can we watch the second one? Please."

"Not tonight," I said. "You have a playdate with Skylar tomorrow, remember?"

"I forgot." She bounced to her feet, her eyes wide with renewed excitement. "And it's like with my birthday. I have to go to sleep for tomorrow to get here."

"That's right." I stroked my hand over her soft hair. "Now, you brush your teeth and get ready for bed."

"Can you read me a story?" Evanne turned those big blue eyes on Lumen. "It's a new one, and Daddy doesn't know it yet."

Lumen looked at me, and I nodded, trying not to let either of them see how much that comment hurt. Not because Evanne had meant anything cruel. When I'd explained my dyslexia to her, she'd offered to help me any time I needed it. No, this was all my issue. I hated the fact that I couldn't pick up any book Evanne wanted and read it to her without extreme difficulty.

I watched Lumen and Evanne go up the stairs and then set about tidying up. It didn't take long, and when I returned to the couch, I started flipping through channels, trying to find something that would distract me.

Jealousy overshadowed all the warmth and contentment of the evening, and I hated it.

I didn't want to be jealous that Lumen could give Evanne something I couldn't. No one could truly be everything to their child. Everyone had strengths and weaknesses, ways they compensated for things they were unable to provide. Unfortunately, that fact didn't make me feel like any less of a failure.

I finally settled on a history special about World War II and tried to get my mind focused on that. I'd only been watching it for ten minutes or so before Lumen came back into the room and sat next to me on the couch. She didn't say anything as she leaned against me, and we watched the rest of the special in silence. Only after it was finished did she speak.

"She doesn't think any less of you, you know that, right?"

I didn't need to ask what Lumen meant. "I know."

She sat up, turning toward me. "I mean it, Alec. To Evanne, you're still the biggest person in her world. The most important. The strongest. The smartest. You are everything to that little girl."

I didn't take my eyes from the television. "Every day, she has people telling her how important it is to be able to read and write. She'll study it all the way to gradua-tion and perhaps even beyond that. And every time she hears someone say how necessary it is, she'll remember that her father struggled to read her children's books."

Lumen put her hand on my cheek and turned my face toward her. "No, Alec. What she'll remember is that you memorized books just so you could tell her the stories. She'll remember that you were open and honest about things that were difficult for you. She will know that you love her more than anything else in this world and that she can come to you with any problem without having to worry about losing that love or disappointing you."

If Keli, or any other woman I'd been with, had said anything like that to me, I would have dismissed it as flattery, pity designed to make me feel better about myself. With Lumen, I realized it would never be that. She would tell the truth, perhaps tactfully, but it would be honest. And never pitying. If anything, she wouldn't allow me to pity myself.

"I love being a teacher."

Before I could wonder at the shift in conversation, she went on to explain.

"But I hate the way education too often confuses knowledge with intelligence. How the way we determine how 'smart' a child is based on subjects the system has deemed the most important, from measurements that have more to do with retention and repetition than anything else. We've created a society where we evaluate a person's worth based on how far they went in formal education, how many letters they have behind their name, their class ranking, or GPA." She reached over and took my hand, threading her fingers between mine. "You are a brilliant man with a first-rate mind. You do things I couldn't even dream of accomplishing. Having a learning disability isn't even the smallest fraction of who you are. It's no more an imperfection than this scar."

She traced the scar that ran through my right eyebrow.

"Some people would consider a scar an imperfection," I said quietly. I wanted to believe her, to think the way she did, but I didn't know if I could get past a lifetime of struggling to see myself as anything but flawed.

"Some people are idiots." She leaned forward and kissed my forehead, right where my scar began. "The parts that make us into the complex, amazing people we are, aren't only the nice and pretty parts. We're so much more than a single piece."

God, I adored this woman, and I didn't even bother to keep what I felt for her off my face. "Have I told you how much I love you?"

"You have." Her smile was the most beautiful I'd ever seen. "But it's always nice to hear it."

"I love you more than words can say." It was my turn

to lean forward and kiss her. I kept it brief, feeling as if she had more to say.

"I love you too." She squeezed my hand. "I've been wanting to ask you this, and it seems like the right time to do it. There have been strides in dealing with dyslexia, even in the time since you were in school. Some techniques, tips, and tricks. They might be able to help you read and write better. I know you have your own system, but maybe these could be incorporated into what you already do or when you're in a situation where something you would normally do just won't work."

For a moment, I remembered all the frustration and shame I'd dealt with every time I was in a situation where I thought my secret would get out. But then I reminded myself that I didn't have to hide any of it from Lumen. And maybe I didn't need to hide it from anyone else either. The first step, though, had to be accepting help.

"Would you be the one teaching those to me?"

She lifted my hand to kiss each of my fingers. "I can if you want. I wasn't sure you'd be comfortable with me in that role."

"I'd prefer to have you do it." I winked at her, suddenly realizing the opportunity that had dropped neatly in my lap. "After all, lass, there are certain *incen-*

tives you can offer that I wouldn't accept from anyone else."

She flushed and laughed. "Why do I have a feeling you already have a few things in mind?"

"Aye, I do." I leaned in and took her lip between my teeth, giving it a tug. "We should probably start right away."

TWENTY-SEVEN
LUMEN

I'd been trying to figure out all week how to approach the idea of me giving Alec some ideas about how to help deal with his dyslexia. Who knew he'd give me a perfect opening? And then a perfect way to ensure he didn't blow it off when we scheduled a time to work on it. I should have known he'd want to get started right away. With the exception of dealing with relationship matters, he didn't procrastinate.

"You know, I'm trying to decide if you're a workaholic or just a glutton for punishment," I said.

"It all depends on who's giving out the punishment." His eyes gleamed as he leaned toward me, his hands sliding up my legs to my thighs.

With Evanne back, things with Keli on track, and his secret about his dyslexia out in the open, it was like a weight had been taken off his shoulders. He still wasn't a laid-back sort of guy, but everything about him just seemed...lighter.

"You don't strike me as the kind of guy who's into getting spanked."

He laughed, and the sound twisted all sorts of things inside me. "No, lass, but I like the idea of having a go at your arse."

I ran my fingers through his hair and leaned toward him until our lips were only a hair's breadth apart. "Maybe my ass could be one of your rewards. Not tonight, but it could be something that you can look forward to."

"I love the way your mind works, lass." His hands slid higher. "What do I get tonight?"

I moved his hands off my lap. "You have to earn it."

"What will I earn?"

I thought for a moment. "The first thing we need to do is go through what you've done so we're not repeating anything. How about for each thing you tell me, I'll take off an article of clothing?"

He raised an eyebrow. "And if I lie just to get you naked?"

"We'll work on the honor system." It was my turn to wink at him.

He chuckled. "Then I need to be on my best behavior."

Ten minutes later, I knew what he'd tried, what worked, and what didn't, and I was naked. And his hand was slowly moving up my thigh...until I slapped it.

"Hands off." I pointed at him. "You haven't earned it yet."

"And how, exactly, do I earn it?" He ran a finger along my shoulder and then across my collarbone.

"That's not hands off." My protest wasn't even half-hearted. His touch made me feel like my skin was on fire. In a good way.

"You're altogether too tempting." He pulled his hands back.

"If you can't pay attention, I'll have to get dressed again," I warned him.

"Quite the motivational threat."

"Now that I know what you've tried, here are a couple other ideas. If you listen to them and agree to try them, I'll have a special reward for you."

"I like the sound of that."

I did too.

"One thing that's been known to help with reading is colored paper," I began going through the mental checklist I'd made. "Different fonts can also make a difference, particularly on a screen."

He nodded, his expression serious despite the nudity going on right in front of him. That was good. It meant he was paying attention. I had no problem making it fun, but I didn't want him to be dismissive.

"My college advisor specialized in teaching students with learning disabilities. He was working on a study using sign language. He reasoned that if spelling words out with sensory-connected techniques like writing the letters in sand, that sort of thing, and learning to identify sight words by shape rather than letter by letter, combining them into one might work just as well since that's how you're taught to read finger spelling, by shape."

He looked appalled. "That means I have to learn a whole new language?"

"Just the alphabet. And I can teach it to you."

He bobbed his eyebrows. "And you'll make it worth my while." It was a statement, not a question.

I slid off the couch and onto my knees, his gaze hot on my skin. I put my hands on his knees and pushed his legs apart. He cursed softly as I moved between them.

"I think I can do that." I reached for his belt, my tongue already out, wetting my lips. "Would you like your reward for listening?"

He cupped my chin and ran his thumb along my bottom lip. "Aye, lass. I'd like that."

As I undid his pants, he reached behind my head and pulled my hair free of my ponytail. The waves spilled over my shoulders, heavy and soft, and somehow more sensual than my hair had ever felt.

"Beautiful, *mo nighean bhan.*"

My fair-haired girl.

I tugged his pants and underwear down enough for his cock to bounce free. Thick and heavy, it curved up toward his stomach. My pussy throbbed, remembering the feel of him inside me. I would wait, though. He came first this time.

I wrapped my hand around the base of his cock, dragging my hand up the length of him and then swiping my thumb across the tip. He made a sound low in his throat, his fingers tightening in my hair. If we'd been in the bedroom, I would have drawn this out, but I was already a little nervous about the possibility of Evanne catching us. I needed to make this quick.

I lowered my head, taking him into my mouth. I closed my lips around him, my tongue swirling around his cock. As I took more of him, I worked my hand up and down on the part I couldn't reach with my mouth. I took him as deep as I could, then sucked hard as I raised my head. He swore, adding in a few words I couldn't understand, but the tone was positive, and that was enough for me.

"Touch yourself," he ordered. "I want you to come too."

I was grateful for the command and reached down to find myself wet. I used my middle two fingers, rubbing my clit back and forth, then in circles. The pressure built rapidly inside me, and I moaned, the sound muffled by the thick shaft moving in and out of my mouth.

When I came, I froze, body stiff as pleasure exploded through me. I didn't stay motionless long, wanting to give him the same. Up and down, I worked my hand and mouth in tandem, increasing suction and friction until Alec's hips started jerking, a sign he was close to losing control.

I used my now free hand to grip his balls, lightly squeezing as I rolled them in my hand. He came less than a minute later, spilling himself across my tongue. I swallowed, then licked him clean before letting him slip out of my mouth.

"Fuck, lass." Alec's voice was rough. "When I can walk again, I'll be taking you to the bedroom to give you a thorough *thank you* for that."

I sat back on my heels, trying to catch my breath. I had a feeling I was going to need it. Despite what we were doing tomorrow, I was willing to bet I wouldn't be getting much sleep tonight, but I was fine with that. I doubted I'd have slept well anyway.

TWENTY-EIGHT
LUMEN

L<small>EAVING</small> A<small>LEC</small> <small>AND GOING BACK HOME FOR THE</small> night had been harder than I'd expected. It was well past midnight, and we'd pretty thoroughly exhausted ourselves physically, but we'd both still had a decent amount on our minds.

Going home had seemed like the best way for us to be able to attempt at least some rest. Especially when I knew he didn't entirely agree with the plan we had in place. The fact that he hadn't tried to talk me out of it or take control of the situation was proof to me of how seriously he was taking our second chance.

Hob and Mai had already been in bed by the time I got home, so I didn't see them until I joined them in the kitchen. The scene looked like any other Saturday morning where Hob was making breakfast for all three of us, but the atmosphere was far from normal.

I had to say something.

"You guys can still bow out. I have Alec and two of his brothers. The four of us can handle things."

Mai glared at me. "Hell no."

"She's right." Hob pointed a spatula at me. "You aren't going in there alone. It's not safe."

"You need me in there with you," Mai continued. "What if he tries something?"

I was tempted to remind her that she wasn't the most physically intimidating person, but I couldn't quite muster the light-hearted tone the comment needed to come across right. As much as I'd been trying to portray optimism and a steadfast belief in our plan, my nerves were stretched to the breaking point. We would succeed because I refuse to let myself consider anything else...no matter how often my brain had wanted to turn that way the past few days.

Any time my thoughts started down a dark path, I remembered what Soleil looked like when I'd found her in the hall and then again when I'd seen her after her suicide attempt. That was always enough to bolster my determination. It also kept me focused on how serious this was, and now that it was time to put things in motion, I was feeling the pressure.

"This is going to work." Mai put her hand on mine. "We can do this."

I nodded, not trusting myself to speak. One way or another, things were going to change today.

I HAD to admit that I'd been a little surprised that Lihua had agreed to let us use Real Life Bodywork to trap a rapist cop. Not because I thought she didn't care about that sort of thing, but because she had always been extremely avid about making sure no one even so much as thought of the business in the same sentence as sex. But when Mai and I had explained what had happened to Soleil, Lihua had simply said that she would help in any way she could.

While it'd been tempting to play up the 'schoolgirl' angle, we had to think about how it would play to a jury. Plain shorts and t-shirts gave us an innocent look that made us both appear younger without us having to worry about provoking jurors. We did our hair in pigtails – mine braided – and did the sort of makeup that young teenage girls did when they wanted to look older.

Neither she nor I could've passed for fourteen, but the costumes and lighting did help us look younger. Our mannerisms would do the rest. Besides, if Clyde thought he was coming in for a 'free *special* massage' being offered to select members of law enforcement, his mind would fill in things to fit those expectations.

At least it would long enough for us to get what we needed from him.

I hoped.

"Please tell me that you feel as nauseous as I do," Mai said as we double-checked the camera placement in the room we were using. "I mean, I'm all for a little role-playing in the bedroom, but this..." She wrinkled her nose, looking pale.

"Is sick, I know," I said quietly. "I don't know how undercover cops do it."

"Sight and sound are good on our end." Eoin's voice came through loud and clear on the coms in Mai and my ears. "If either of you want out, now's the time to say it. We can still cancel."

"Not a chance." My voice was firm. "I want this bastard behind bars."

"What she said," Mai added.

"Do you both remember your signal word if you're in trouble?" Alec was trying to sound as at ease as his brother, but I could hear the tense undercurrent.

"Scream 'we're in trouble?'" Mai joked.

"Mai." Hob's voice was gentle. He knew, like I did, that this was how Mai dealt with stress.

"Sorry." She took a deep breath. "It's *heat*."

"As in 'should I turn up the heat in here?'" I added. "We both remember."

"Good," Eoin said. "Brody, we haven't heard from you yet. Check your coms."

"Loud and clear." Brody's voice came through my earpiece. "Before we really get started, little brother, I'd love to know when you learned how to do all this surveillance shit. I thought you were a grunt, not a spy."

"When I was stationed stateside after my first tour, a couple intelligence guys came in for a couple days. I kept in touch with one of them, and I reached out when Lumen told me what she wanted to do. Cain knows his shit."

"And I'm glad he does," I said, feeling the knot in my stomach loosening a bit with this new knowledge.

I'd made the right decision, going to him. Eoin knew what he was doing. Not just the logistical stuff, but being calm and in control. He didn't blow off the danger of what we were doing but didn't let emotion get in the way. I loved Alec and valued his qualities, but Eoin was the McCrae with the skills I needed to pull this off.

"All right. Get in place. The mark just pulled into the parking lot." Eoin's voice was steady as he relayed the information. "Hob, are you ready?"

"To take a serial rapist into a room with my girlfriend and one of my closest friends for a massage? Not really."

"Hob." It was Mai's turn to pull Hob back in.

"Yes, I'm ready."

"Good." Eoin paused and then said, "Incoming."

Mai and I moved over to the massage table, putting it between us and the door. I clasped my hands behind my back and saw Mai do the same. It was a good way to keep our hands from shaking…and it kept me from hitting Clyde when he walked into the room a minute later.

Just under six feet tall, Clyde had an athletic build, which meant this was a little more dangerous than if he'd been some overweight, over-the-hill stereotype. Despite the thinning hair that was either dark blond or light brown, and muddy brown eyes that slithered over me and then moved on to Mai, he was a decent-looking guy. Or would have been if I hadn't known what a horrible person he truly was.

"Hello there, sweet things."

If I hadn't felt like I wanted to throw up before, I definitely did now. The man oozed sleaze.

"Hello," Mai and I chorused together.

Mai held out the usual paperwork that came with scheduling an appointment and when he took the clipboard, I half-expected him to actually fill things out and completely screw up the sting. Instead, he tossed it on the chair by the door.

"I don't think we need to worry about names. This is just between us."

He licked his lips and started unbuttoning his shirt. I only just then realized that he was still wearing his uniform. The bastard wasn't even trying to hide the fact that he was a cop.

"You two gonna help me undress?" His leer made my skin crawl.

Mai and I exchanged glances, both of us trying to look coy. She was managing the sex kitten act much better than me, but I was doing my best.

"Stay calm," Eoin said softly. "Act unsure. Shy."

Clyde tossed his shirt on the empty chair next to the door. "Fine by me if you don't talk. I don't care much for chatter. In my opinion, a girl's mouth is only good for one thing, and talking's not it."

When he started on his pants, I was tempted to tell him I definitely did *not* want to see what he had underneath his briefs, but I hadn't come here to give up just because I didn't want to see his dick.

And what a sad-looking dick it was too.

I nearly laughed when he straightened, hands on hips as if he should be proud of the ratty nest of pubic hair surrounding a limp couple inches of thin flesh. Then he cupped himself and mercifully hid it from sight. He ignored the towel sitting right in front of him on the table.

"Like what you see, sweet thing?" When I didn't answer, he laughed before asking, "How's this work?"

"Lay down on your stomach, and we'll start with your back," I said, taking a step forward.

"And when do we get to the happy ending?"

"At the end, of course," Mai said, moving up next to me with a smile.

"How about we just skip to the end then?" He climbed on the table and laid down on his back, folding his hands behind his head. "I mean, it is supposed to be something *special,* right? I'm in charge."

For a moment, I had this utterly surreal sense of déjà vu. Or, rather, the upside-down version of déjà vu where my memory of Alec laying on my table overlapped with this one. The near-instant attraction I'd felt toward him. How I'd wondered about what had been under the towel covering a clear erection.

This experience was the exact opposite of that one.

"Aren't you girls going to get more comfortable?" He wiggled his hips, and his penis flopped around. It looked like it was a little harder than before, but I didn't really want to examine it any closer.

"Are you asking us to undress for your massage?" I worded the question carefully. "That isn't included in today's package."

"Is that included in another package?" he asked, annoyance in his voice. "And why didn't I get that one?"

Alec had gotten advice from an attorney about our 'hypothetical' situation, and we'd scripted questions accordingly. The last thing we wanted was Clyde to go free because we'd left room for interpretation.

"Are you stupid or something?" He propped himself up on his elbows. "Take off your clothes."

"We're coming in," Alec's voice came over the com.

"No, we're not," Eoin quickly cut in. "We're waiting for the signal."

"We only know what we're told," I said, trying to ignore the men's voices. "If we add anything, we'll get in trouble."

"You're gonna be in trouble with me, and trust me, you don't want that," he warned.

"Do you want to see another package?" Mai asked. "It's not much more."

He sighed. "Fine. How much more?"

Mai and I exchanged looks. I answered the question. "Twenty?"

"Fine. I'll give it to you after."

"Okay. While we're undressing, why don't you tell us what you'd like us to do for your massage," Mai said.

"How about you two undress each other, just to get my imagination going?"

This time, it was Hob who spoke in our ears. "I'm going to kill him."

"I'd think a strong, handsome guy like you knows exactly what to do with girls like us." The words almost choked me on their way out of my mouth, but we needed to get enough on tape before he took things too far.

"I have a few ideas," he said as he sat up. He wrapped his hand around his cock. "First, let's see those titties."

I heard curses in four different voices. Clyde was lucky we had a camera on because I had a feeling that was pretty much the only thing keeping the guys from coming in and beating him within an inch of his life.

Since my outfit had a buttoned blouse, it would buy us more time. Mai and I exchanged one of those looks that only people who are really close could understand. She gave me a minute nod and reached for my top button.

"Are you wearing bras?" Clyde asked.

"Yes," I answered for both of us. "Pretty white lace."

"I like the sound of that. Let me see."

When we were done here, I was going to throw up.

Mai's fingers shook as she made it halfway down my shirt, but the fire in her eyes told me it was from anger rather than fear.

"I have to ask, are you girls bare down there? I like pussies baby smooth. Feels good on my cock."

Yeah, I was definitely going to throw up.

"If not, you can hire a new girl. Younger so they don't even need to shave."

My blouse was completely open in the front now, but I'd picked my bra specifically with this sort of scenario in mind. I was as covered as I would've been in a bikini. Not that it made me any more comfortable, but it was something.

"How young?" I asked as I took a step toward him, putting Mai behind him. "I mean, we're not *old*."

Clyde's eyes narrowed. "You ask an awful lot of questions for a whore. When I pay for a mouth, I want it sucking my dick, not talking."

"We just want to know what you want," Mai spoke up from behind me. "I mean, you *are* in charge."

For a moment, I thought she'd mollified him, but then he stood up, a scowl on his face. "What's going on here? You better not be trying to shake me down or something like that." He took a step toward us, reaching toward me.

I didn't jump back fast enough and he grabbed my

arm. Shit. "Um, is it cold in here? Because I can turn up the heat if you want."

"What the fuck are you trying to sa—" The last word was cut off as the door burst open and Eoin grabbed Clyde from behind, startling the cop enough that he dropped my arm.

Mai and I dove for the farthest corner of the room as Eoin slammed Clyde into the wall face first. The other guys came in only a couple seconds behind, and the anger on Alec's and Hob's faces made me wonder if Brody had kept them back those few moments in order for Eoin to contain the perverted bastard.

Alec took a step toward Clyde, eyes flashing, hands in fists.

"Alec!" I grabbed his arm. "Please."

He looked down at me, and I saw that rage wasn't the only thing in his eyes. For the first time, I realized what it must have been like for him, sitting and watching, not defending me or protecting me from that awful man. I wrapped my arms around his waist, breathing a sigh of relief when he returned my embrace.

"Never again, lass. Please." He kissed the top of my head. "I canna take that again."

"Don't worry." My voice was shaky. "I don't plan on making a career change. I fully intend to go back to being a mild-mannered teacher from here on out."

He chuckled, his arms tightening around me.

"The police are on their way," Brody announced.

Clyde started laughing. "You guys are so fucked. You don't even know how bad. I've got you for entrapment and solicitation and assault–"

"Shut up." Eoin deposited Clyde in a chair.

I pulled out of Alec's hug but kept one arm around his waist as I turned toward Clyde. "No, you're the one who doesn't realize how badly *you're* fucked."

"It's your word against mine," he said. "I'll tell them how I just came here for a massage, and the two of you started undressing and offering all sorts of sexual favors."

"We have you on camera." Hob was the one who spoke this time. I'd never seen my normally laid-back friend this furious.

Clyde seemed to deflate. "What?"

Mai walked over to where we'd hidden the camera and pulled it out. "Everything that happened from the moment you walked in here has been recorded. And before you start making threats about losing evidence or whatever, it's backed up online."

"You won't get away with this. I have friends in high places." He leaned forward like he was going to stand up, but one look from Eoin had Clyde huddling back in his seat.

Mai planted her hands on her hips. "Is it just me, or

does he sound like one of those villains from *Scooby-Doo?*"

"I must have forgotten to mention that I made a call as well," Alec said. "Prosecutor Jefferson George and I have known each other for years. He should be here about the same time as the police."

"Son of a bitch!" Clyde stamped both of his feet on the floor like a child throwing a tantrum. "You can't do this to me! I'm a cop!"

I moved closer until I was just out of his reach. "A cop who repeatedly raped his girlfriend's teenage daughter."

All the color drained from his face, then rushed back to turn his skin an unhealthy shade of red. "That little bitch! No one will believe her!"

"Maybe not," I moved a step closer, "but how long do you think it'll take at least one of your buddies to sell you out in exchange for a deal? We've got DNA and pictures of what she looked like when they were done with her. Former cops who gang-raped a fourteen-year-old won't last long in prison."

I stopped when he began to hyperventilate. For Soleil's sake, I didn't want this to go to trial. Clyde needed to take a plea, and I hoped that the seed I'd just planted would get the desired results. No matter what he did, however, he'd never touch another girl again. I'd make sure of it.

"Police!" The shout came from the lobby.

"I've got it." Brody hurried out of the room.

"Here, lass," Alec said, draping his coat over me. "They'll probably want to note what you're wearing before they let you change. Let's get this over with."

I nodded, breathing easier as Alec's scent surrounded me. The day wasn't done yet, but we'd done the hard part already. Now, I had to trust that the system would do its job. It wasn't easy, having grown up seeing the things that people could get away with, but I had to have hope, otherwise, what was the point?

———

I COULD HAVE DONE this alone, but I wanted Alec to come, not only because he'd helped with Clyde getting arrested, but because Brie's house had been an important part of my life, and still was. Alec couldn't truly understand me if he didn't understand the things that made me who I was.

"Just a warning," I said as he parked the car in the group home driveway. "Some of the kids may freak out a little. I've never brought anyone here before."

"Never?" He gave me a surprised look. "What about Mai?"

I shook my head. "Not even Mai." I paused, gathering my thoughts before speaking again. "She knows pretty much what you know. That I was raised in foster care. This is the last group home I was ever in. Brie, the foster mom, treated me with respect, prepared me for aging out. It's why I come back, to show the kids that they can have a future, a home, a career."

"That's how you met Soleil," he said.

"It is." I reached over and took his hand. "I'm not ashamed of having grown up here, but bringing someone here, letting them see..."

"It's personal." His free hand came up and brushed back my hair. "I understand."

If anyone could understand wanting to keep some things private, it was the man who'd hidden his dyslexia from everyone outside of his family.

"Just, if they make a big deal out of it, that's why."

"Do you want me to stay in the car? Whatever you want, I will do." He took both of my hands and kissed my knuckles.

"No, I'd like you to come in and meet everyone."

It was time for me to stop putting up walls. I had people who loved me, and they deserved to know all of me. I didn't have any delusions that this was going to be easy or that it would happen all at once. It would be a process, and I'd have to work at it, but it was time.

TWENTY-NINE
ALEC

COMPLETE AND UTTER CHAOS.

Squared.

There was no other description that could come closer to accurately portraying a birthday party for an eight-year-old girl who had a massive extended family and an entire third-grade class full of friends. It was halfway through November, which meant we were all inside. My house was big enough to handle it, but it was a close thing.

Still, as I turned quickly to avoid yet another collision with a small child, I wondered if it had been a good idea to have both family and friends over all at once. I wouldn't say a word about it, though. Not when Lumen had suggested two separate parties, and I'd said I could handle it.

I'd managed multi-billion dollar deals with people whose language I didn't know. How hard could it be to plan a birthday party?

The answer to that was a resounding *I had no idea.* I'd actually made a point to reach out to Keli two days ago to ask her for advice since she'd been the one to plan these sorts of parties before. Granted, she'd always had enough sense not to combine them, but she'd offered some bits of advice that had helped things run more smoothly today. She'd actually spoken nicely to Lumen more than once as well. It was encouraging.

"She's lovely." Theresa came up beside me.

I didn't need to ask for clarification to know Mom wasn't talking about my ex.

"She is," I agreed. "Smart, sweet...all the things I don't deserve."

Theresa put her hand on my arm, and I looked down at her. "Maybe I didn't tell you this enough growing up, but you are a good man, Alec McCrae. A great father. You're smart and loyal and a dozen other wonderful things that you don't recognize about yourself."

Emotion tightened my chest. "Thank you, Mom."

She reached up and gave me a hug. "I'll go make sure the right number of candles are on the cake."

And that was Theresa's not-so-subtle way of saying she still didn't trust Keli, not even to do something as simple as put the right number of candles on a cake. My family's opinion of Keli had made me more than a little nervous about them meeting Lumen, but not inviting Lumen wasn't an option. She was my future.

A future that began with a pretty blonde teacher and my dark-haired future track star. The latter was chattering excitedly with Skylar about the field trip the third graders were taking the day before Thanksgiving break. As for the former...my eyes automatically scanned the room for Lumen, drawn to her the way I had been from the first time I'd seen her.

She was standing with Eoin and Aspen, but as if she felt my gaze on her, she looked up. Her eyes met mine, and a bolt of desire went straight through me. Her eyes darkened, and I saw everything I felt reflected in those bright blue depths.

Later, she mouthed.

That was a promise I was going to hold her to, but at the moment, I had candles to light.

When I walked into the kitchen, both Keli and Theresa were standing at the counter, neither one looking overly happy at the other one's presence. On the counter was a beautiful cake decorated with a picture of a cheetah princess. According to Lumen, Evanne had introduced her classmates to playing 'cheetah princesses and princes' at recess. When I'd asked Evanne about it, she'd launched into a long and detailed explanation that I'd barely been able to follow. What I had understood was how excited she was about it.

"Keli, would you gather everyone around the table? I'll carry the cake out when you start them singing."

"Of course." Her smile was a little tight, but she was still trying.

We'd come to a custody agreement more easily than I'd expected, leading me to add an addendum that we'd revisit the arrangement in six months. It had only been a few days, but I was optimistic.

"Happy birthday to you..."

I finished lighting the candles and then carried the cake into the dining room. There, sitting at the head of the table was my beaming daughter, clapping her hands in excitement at the sight of her cake. I set it down carefully and then moved to stand behind her, Keli on the other side. As the song finished, everyone cheered for her to blow out the nine candles on her cake. She got them all in a single breath.

When Keli looked at me, I motioned for her to cut the cake. I leaned down and kissed Evanne's head. "I'm going to get the cupcakes."

With a party of this size, one cake would only have been enough if it had been half the size of the table itself. We'd compromised. A sheet cake with her cheetah princess decoration and then four dozen cupcakes with candy tiaras. Lumen had originally offered to make the cupcakes, and then I'd told her how many we needed. Needless to say, she'd rescinded the offer.

By the time I got to the kitchen, Lumen was already there, taking the lid off the cupcake trays. Her back was to me, and it was far too tempting to put my hands on her. I slid my arms around her waist and pulled her back against me. The light vanilla scent she wore mingled with the sweet smell of the cupcakes, making me hungry in more than one way.

"You don't need to do that, lass." I kissed the top of her head.

"I want to." She leaned back against me. "You did an amazing job on this party."

"Thank you."

"And as much as I'd like to spend a little more time alone with you, I think we should get these cupcakes out there before the vultures descend."

I chuckled. "I was thinking along the same lines."

"I'll take this tray, and you take that one."

Before I released her, I had one question I needed to ask. "How are you doing? I know my family can be a bit much."

She turned in my arms and stretched up to kiss my

cheek. "They're great. I've talked to all of them, and they've been amazing."

"Not too amazing, though?" I was only half-joking. I knew all too well how most women reacted to the men in my family.

"Are you jealous, Mr. McCrae?" she teased.

"Just a wee bit," I admitted.

"Don't be. I only have eyes for you." She brushed her lips across mine and then stepped away, picking up the tray of cupcakes.

After cake and ice cream, it was time for presents, keeping me busy until Evanne finished thanking everyone and then asked if she could start playing with some of her new toys. Only then was I able to step away for a few minutes of quiet and solitude. Except when I went into the library, Eoin was already there.

"A little too much for you too?" I asked.

He shrugged. "Noise bugs me sometimes."

I nodded as if I understood a fraction of what he'd been through even though I knew that wasn't possible. "Thank you again for all the help you've given us this past week."

"I'm glad I was able to help." He walked over to the window, but I got the impression he wasn't really looking at anything. "It was good to feel like I was doing some good again."

I felt like he was more talking to himself than to me, but I listened anyway. The more time I'd spent with him this week, the more I'd seen how much he was struggling.

"I've been thinking I might want to do something like private security or private investigating." He rubbed the back of his neck. "Is that stupid?"

"Not at all," I said, meaning it. "Anything I can do to help, just say the word."

He nodded. "I will."

Any other conversation was pushed aside when half a dozen kids came running into the library, waving what appeared to be aluminum foil swords.

I looked over at Eoin, and we both said the same thing.

"Brody."

THIRTY

LUMEN

CHRISTMAS EVE - ONE YEAR LATER

Sixteen months and two weeks. That was how long I'd known Alec. Not quite a year and a half, and I still could barely believe that this was my life.

Growing up, I'd been by myself, and even when I'd gone to live with Brie, I'd always been painfully aware that what I'd had hadn't been a family. At least, not the way I'd always pictured a family to be.

Then I'd met Mai, and the Jins had welcomed me into their lives. I hadn't been alone, but I'd still felt like an intruder. Now, after more than a year with Alec, my outlook had changed.

It was one thing to understand the blended family

dynamic from a factual standpoint, but it was something else entirely to go to Thanksgiving in San Ramon and see it personally. To them, it didn't matter how any of them were connected by blood or whether or not they referred to Patrick and Theresa by their first names or as Mom and Da. Half, step, cousin, adopted, biological.

Those were only descriptive words on the same level as "oldest" or "youngest" or "the baby." They even jokingly referred to themselves as the "Grace families," since a quirk of fate had merged families whose last names had similar meanings. Fate. Destiny. Whoever or whatever had brought everyone together. It didn't matter. They were a family because they chose to be.

So, I'd chosen too. I'd chosen Alec and Evanne and the rest of their family. Even in some way, I'd chosen Keli even though we'd never be friends. And I'd chosen Soleil.

I scanned the room for her and smiled when I saw her talking to the youngest of Alec's siblings, his half-sister, London. The entire family was gorgeous, and none more so than the actress with the long, strawberry blonde curls and brandy-colored eyes. Soleil had been star-struck from moment one, and London was about as far from a snob or diva as anyone could get. And London wasn't the only celebrity in the family either.

Brody made several top-shelf whiskeys. The older of the fraternal McCrae twins, Carson, was a much-sought-after fashion designer. In fact, he'd put together my entire outfit for tonight, from the black cocktail dress to the peep-toe pumps and clutch handbag.

His younger brother, Cory, and their step-cousin slash adopted brother, Fury Gracen, founded their own marketing and investment company. Maggie played the violin in the New York Philharmonic. The identical McCrae twins, Sean and Xander, were a motivational speaker and a premier soccer player, respectively.

Austin Carideo was much like Alec when it came to business, though the company his late father had founded was based in technology. Rome Carideo was a real estate developer. The family referred to Paris as the female Indiana Jones while Aspen's travels were due to her freelance art restoration firm.

Blaze Gracen was a professor of Education at Johns Hopkins University, and his baby sister, Rose, was working toward owning her own horse breeding ranch.

And I was a third-grade teacher.

My first Thanksgiving with them had intimidated the hell out of me. Without the chaos of Evanne's class-mates like I'd had at the birthday party, much of the attention had been focused on me, especially after Alec had announced that I'd applied to be a foster parent. I'd learned quickly that they prized family above all else, and my willingness to foster a teenager had won them over completely.

Everything had been in flux this past year, not only because my relationship with Alec was deepening. At Thanksgiving last year, Hob and Mai had gotten engaged. Two weeks later, Mai had moved in with him, and Soleil had come to live with me.

Shortly after the first of the year, Soleil's mother had signed off on my adopting the girl. The weekend after the adoption had been finalized, Soleil and I had moved in with Alec and Evanne. If Soleil had expressed the slightest reluctance, we would have stayed at the apartment, but she'd become attached to Evanne from the first time the two of them had met and had been thrilled at the chance to be a full-time big sister.

One thing I'd been worried about through the entire process was Keli, but she'd actually been great. Things had gotten better enough that Alec had redone the custody arrangement to a two-week swap with alternating holidays. Keli hadn't even minded that Evanne had taken to calling me Mama L. It still tugged at my heart every time I heard it.

"Any particular reason you're hiding back here?"

Eoin came up beside me. "Usually, I'm the one keeping to the shadows."

Over the past year, I'd grown quite fond of Alec's younger brother. He'd been through a lot.

"I'm just thinking about how lucky I am." I accepted the glass of eggnog he held out. "It still feels like a dream sometimes."

Eoin nodded his head in understanding. "When life throws you curveballs all the time, sometimes you don't know what to do with the easy lob."

"Baseball reference?" I gave him a sideways look. "Really?"

He grinned and shrugged. "What can I say? I've got layers."

As he rejoined the party, I felt someone step up behind me. An arm slid around my waist, and even if I hadn't seen the Vacheron Constantin watch on his wrist, I would have known it was Alec. I could feel him in a way that went beyond the simple press of his body against mine.

"Let's say our farewells. The driver's waiting, and the plane is ready to take us home." His voice was low in my ear. "I have something I want to give you after the girls go to sleep."

I nodded, not trusting my voice to be steady. His touch made me weak in the knees, and that promise of a gift had my thoughts racing. The two-hour flight home was going to be the best sort of torture.

"WE'RE NOT ALLOWED to wake Daddy and Mama L up until six o'clock," Evanne explained solemnly as she and Soleil carried a plate of cookies into the living room and set it on the table next to the tree. "Or else we have to wait until after breakfast to open presents."

"Then we better make sure we pay attention to the clock." Soleil didn't crack a smile, but when she glanced up at me, humor danced in her eyes.

She'd come a long way since her assault and suicide attempt last year, and Evanne had a lot to do with it. Spending time together gave Soleil an opportunity to do childish things that she had missed in her own childhood, but in such a way that she didn't need to be self-conscious about them.

Not having to worry about a trial had also helped. Clyde had been so arrogant after his arrest that, despite being Mirandized and asking to see his department rep, he hadn't stopped talking. He'd been set up. Framed. Mai and I had lured him there under false pretenses, and then he'd been assaulted by a scarred thug. We'd tried to blackmail him.

At that point, his department rep had shown up, but even he hadn't been able to stop Clyde from bringing up the other accusations that he had been certain we had already been making. In his zeal to declare his innocence, he'd provided the police with a list of reasons why we and Soleil had been lying. Unfortunately for him, he'd ended up giving them details that he would have only known had he actually committed the crimes.

It hadn't taken long for the police to arrest the other men who'd assaulted Soleil, and Alec's friend, Jefferson George, had played all of them off each other. With Soleil's permission, he'd used her case to offer all four men various plea deals in exchange for information on the others. While the men would only serve ten to twelve years for what they'd done to her, Jefferson had gathered a plethora of information and charged them with enough crimes to keep them in jail for the rest of their lives.

Soleil hadn't needed to testify or go over what they'd done. Instead, she'd had professional help coming to terms with what had happened. She still had her bad days, but we'd turned a corner, and she was looking forward to the rest of her life. A life I knew would be amazing.

"We also have to go to bed right away," Evanne

continued to explain the Christmas ritual. "Because if we don't, Santa won't come."

"I see," Soleil said, looking very solemn. "Do you think he'd mind if I read you a story?"

"Of course not." Evanne came over to me and motioned for me to bend down. When I did, she whispered loudly in my ear, "I know Santa's not real, but we should pretend for my big sis."

Surprise, amusement, and pride mixed and stirred something deep inside my heart. "That's very sweet of you."

"Don't tell Daddy I know. It'll make him sad. I'll tell him after Christmas."

If I hadn't known how tender Evanne's heart was, I might've thought she was simply angling to get more gifts, but Alec typically kept the 'Santa' gifts small, not wanting other kids to wonder why Evanne would get expensive gifts from Santa when they didn't.

Evanne enjoyed getting gifts, but she wasn't a selfish child. Or a manipulative one. She had no problem boldly stating what she wanted. I had no doubt her revelation to Alec about not believing in Santa would include reasons why she should still get the same number of gifts.

When Alec first brought up the idea of Soleil and me moving in with him, I'd been worried about how Evanne would feel about suddenly having this teenager coming into her house. But when Alec and I had sat her down to talk to her about it, she'd simply said that she'd always wanted a sister. She also said that Soleil was better than a baby because Evanne wouldn't have to wait until the baby was older for them to be able to play together. They'd practically been inseparable ever since.

"You don't mind reading to her?" I asked Soleil.

"Not at all." She smiled. "She doesn't ask for bedtime stories much anymore."

That was true. Over the last year, Evanne had moved to reading chapter books to us rather than us reading stories to her, but more often lately, she'd wanted to read on her own. She was growing up.

"And don't worry, as soon as I'm done, I plan on showering and turning in. Can't be the one who keeps Santa away." Soleil's smile grew even bigger, and it was beautiful to see. "Don't you two stay up too late. I have a feeling we'll be knocking on your door right at six."

I winked at her. "Fair warning, she'll probably wake you up earlier than that."

"I figured as much," she said with a laugh. "All right, squirt. Let's go."

Evanne grabbed Soleil's hand. "Come on. I think we can finish the last two chapters of *Philosopher's Stone* tonight."

"I still don't get why you call it that," Soleil said as she and Evanne headed for the stairs.

"Because Daddy says it's the real title, and that's why he bought me the real book," Evanne explained.

I looked over at Alec, who shrugged.

"It's the truth," he said.

As the girls disappeared upstairs, I walked over to the plate of sugar cookies and picked one up. Soleil and Evanne had iced them all by themselves earlier today, which was how we'd ended up with a red star, a blue Christmas tree, and a purple candy cane.

"I finished up wrapping their Santa gifts while they were doing the cookies," I said before taking a bite. The colors might have been a little off, but they tasted great.

"Thank you, lass." He came over for his own cookie. "When I attempt to wrap a gift, I get caught up in trying to make it perfect and..." He made a motion to indicate that things just kept going.

"Aye, I ken it well," I teased, my horrible attempt at a Scottish accent making him laugh. "I'm glad to do it. I enjoy gift wrapping."

"You are an odd one." He kissed my temple. "After we bring out the girls' gifts, I think we should exchange at least one gift each tonight."

"I like that idea." I'd been trying to think of a tactful way to suggest something similar. From the looks Alec had been giving me when he talked about my Christmas presents, I had a feeling at least one of my gifts would not be anything I'd want either of the girls to see.

"Shall we?"

Finishing my cookie, I followed him to the gift closet. Yes, we had a closet that was set aside specifically for gifts. With a lock. I'd learned that Alec took preserving surprises very seriously.

Once we had everything set out for the morning, Alec poured us both some hot cocoa, and we each selected a single gift from under the tree. I'd considered giving him one of the gifts that related to this one, but now that I could give him something without an audience, I found that I wanted to see his genuine reaction, untampered by what the girls might think.

"You first, lass," he said. "I have a feeling we'll be a wee bit distracted after you open what I have for you."

Definitely skimpy lingerie or a toy.

I held out a thin, flat package. "There's a theme that goes with this and your other gifts, but you only get to open this one tonight."

Alec had become much more open over the last year, and I enjoyed seeing the curiosity and joy that came with opening my gift. He took out a tablet, confusion on his face.

"Before you try to figure out how to thank me for a tablet when you already have two, turn it on."

He did, and then his eyes widened. "Camping at Yosemite National Park?"

"I set up a reservation for nine days for all four of us in June, and I already checked with Keli to make sure the time was over Evanne's two weeks with us." I studied his face, wondering if I'd just proven that I didn't know him as well as I thought I did.

"It's perfect." He leaned forward and kissed me. "Thank you, lass."

He took another minute to look through the information I'd uploaded onto the tablet – specifically formatted to make it easier for him to read – and then set it aside. When he faced me again, his expression was serious.

"Lumen, *mo luaidh*, I will forever be grateful for the mistake that led me to you. My life, my daughter's life... we are better for knowing you." He reached behind him and produced a small box, and my heart began dancing in my chest. "We want you to be a part of our lives forever. You and Soleil. We want the four of us to become a family. Will you marry me?"

He opened the box, and I stared at the ring nestled on black velvet. An oval diamond surrounded by smaller ones. A platinum band with more small diamonds. I blinked, not quite believing my eyes.

"Say something, lass." Alec's voice was uncertain, and that was enough to snap me out of my daze.

"Yes." I cupped his face between my hands and kissed him. "A thousand times, yes."

He took my hand and slid the ring onto my finger. Like everything with Alec, it felt right, as if it belonged there.

"There's one other thing before we celebrate." He licked his lips, looking nervous. "When I said I want you and Soleil as my family, I meant that I want to adopt her as well. But I didn't want to say anything to her before speaking to you."

I didn't think I could possibly love this man any more than I already did, but my heart swelled with more love than I knew how to process.

"She will be thrilled," I said, kissing him again, harder this time. "You know this just makes me love you even more, right?"

He cupped the back of my head and lowered his mouth to mine. Heat flowed through me as he took the kiss deeper. Everything else faded into the background as he pulled me onto his lap. His hands moved to my hips, sliding under the bottom of my dress to palm my bare ass. I moaned into his mouth, and his fingers dug into my flesh.

"Inside you." He bit my bottom lip. "Fuck, lass, I need to be inside you."

"Yes. Yes."

I reached down between us and had him in my hand a few moments later. Then he was moving my panties, and I was lifting up, and the tip of him brushed against me, and then I was sinking down and...

Oh...so good.

We moved together, fast and desperate, chasing our mutual satisfaction. His forehead pressed against mine, and I grabbed the front of his shirt. Small, needy whimpers fell from my mouth, but I couldn't seem to stop. Not that I wanted to. Him filling me. Rubbing against all the right places. Strong hands and hot skin. His ring on my finger. The promise of forever.

"Come for me, lass." Alec's brogue was thick. "Come for me here, and then I'll take you to bed and make love with you all night."

"Yes, please," I whispered.

My eyes squeezed close, and a wave of pleasure rolled over me. I rode it, swallowing my cry as ecstasy flooded every cell, ran across every nerve. Then Alec was holding me tight, driving up into me with two short thrusts before giving himself over to his own release. He groaned my name, pressing his face to the side of my neck. I wrapped my arms around him and rested my cheek on the top of his head.

We'd need to move soon, but for the moment, I was content where I was. For the first time in my life, I felt like I could stop moving, stop searching. I'd found what I'd been looking for.

Home.

THE END

Hope you enjoyed Lumen and Alec's story. Look out for more Scottish Billionaires in the near future.

OFFICE ROMANCES BY M. S. PARKER

The Boss

The Dom

The Master

Chasing Perfection

Unlawful Attraction

A Legal Affair

The Pleasure Series

Serving HIM

The Billionaire's Muse

Bound

One Night Only

Damage Control

Pure Lust Box Set

Printed in Great Britain
by Amazon

47595123R00153